FUEL & FIRE

BURNOUT BOOK TWO

ADELL RYAN

Published by Upside Down Red Umbrella
First Edition: September 2020

Cover Art by Covers by Christian
Edited by G. Surley

CHAPTER ONE

Crow

As soon as Hayes's bedroom door closed behind me, I regretted everything: Slipping the ticket into her shorts; Stroking my cock while Hayes was balls deep inside her and her fist worked Trenton; Watching my cum run down all that smooth, perfect skin…

…How much I enjoyed every damn second.

The tattoos on my fingers stretch as I white-knuckle the steering wheel. Their constant reminder of why this club is so important to me — to the community — comes rushing back. My chest tightens with the threat of another attack.

Taking a deep breath, I convince myself that giving her the ticket was the right thing to do. If someone is out to fuck up what I worked so hard to build, they need to be weeded out stat.

I wanted to give her the ticket and be done. Participating was not part of the plan. But I was fucking spiraling, and Remi was part of the reason. I needed the image of crushed metal and the scent of burnt rubber erased from my mind. A release stolen from her seemed like a perfectly acceptable cure at the time.

Problem is, now I can't fucking get *that* image out of my mind. Hayes and Trenton should have kicked me out of there as soon as I walked in. Watching her simply wasn't enough.

Imagining it was her hand sliding up and down my cock instead of feeling my own, calloused one will never be enough.

The moment I stepped inside and the air, thick with the heat and dampness of her arousal, crashed over me, I was ruined. Getting involved only made matters worse.

Clearly, I need to set better boundaries. Practice a bit more fucking control of my own actions.

Add grief to the mix, and the result is often disastrous. But that is the thing about grief: if you don't lose yourself in something, the grief will chew you up, swallow, regurgitate, and spit you out.

Grief is a dangerous, controlling emotion. The worst of them all.

Tonight, its claws are buried deep inside me and it's not at all remedied by earlier activities, but worsened.

Desperate to regain even a hint of control, I now find myself sitting in my car, watching people walk in and out of the hospital's automatic sliding doors.

Porter is a threat.

To me.

To my friends.

To the club.

To Remi.

Him crashing wasn't enough repayment for the piece of shit that he is. Porter is due for one more unexpected surprise tonight.

A friendly visit.

And thanks to some inside sources, I know exactly where to find him.

I leave my vehicle, prowl inside, and slink my way down hallways and up stairs, keeping against the walls in an attempt to go unnoticed by hospital staff, until the only thing separating us is a curtain.

Why the fuck am I here?

His treatment of Remi has nothing to do with me.

Go home, Burke.

No.

You're not doing this for Remi.

This is for the club.

You'll do well to remember that.

The ink across my knuckles flashes in my line of sight, serving as one more stark reminder when I push the curtain aside.

Porter is lying on the hospital bed, sleeping like a damn baby. I sit down in that convenient bedside chair for visitors, prop my forearms on my thighs, and clasp my hands. Blending in with the dark room, I study every cut on his face from the impact, deciding which one I am about to bust back open.

Once I feel pretty good with my choice, I lean back in the chair and begin a steady tapping on the tight, fake leather of the armrest.

Tap.

Tap.

Tap.

Tap.

Tap.

Tap.

Porter stirs.

Tap.

Tap.

His eyes open and his head angles in my direction.

In a blink, he shoots upward. I stand, pull my fist back, and hit him square on the cheek — right where he had marked Remi. The cut caused by the crash splits back open and blood flows down his face.

Still a bit hazy from pain meds and sleep, he stumbles off the bed and tries to gain footing. I grip the material of his hospital gown at the neck and pull him toward me. "Lay a hand on her again or run on my streets, and your car and face won't be the only things that get fucked up."

He straightens, chin back. "If I were you, I'd go ahead and work on an apology," he says bringing his fingers up to the cut and pulling them back to eye the amount of blood. "You're not ready to play with the big boys yet."

Like the pansy asshole he is, Porter bends down and presses the *Nurse Call* button on the remote. I yank my hand away, simultaneously pushing him back onto the bed.

"Stay in your lane," I growl in warning before storming out.

CHAPTER TWO

Remi

After getting dressed last night, I remembered that we had decided I would stay here instead of going home. Hayes had offered me a shirt to sleep in. When I asked Trenton for his mesh shorts, he politely declined, explaining that he much prefers me to sleep without shorts, for "easier access" and all.

As soon as Hayes, Trenton, and I were all cleaned up after the insanely incredible threesome — foursome? — we fell hard and fast in a mix of limbs on the bed.

Not including Crow, of course.

He left faster than he… came.

An ever-so-slight increase in breathing pace under my hand is enough to stir me awake hours later. When my eyes flutter open, the room is still bathed in a purple glow. Blackout curtains over the windows refuse any hint as to the time of day.

Head still nestled in the crook of Hayes's arm and slightly propped up on his shoulder, I adjust to peer up at him. He gives me a tired smile, brings his hand to my shoulder, and runs lazy fingers down my forearm.

"Good morning," he whispers.

The sleepy rasp in his tone causes an unfair blush to spread across over my face. Unable to hold his piercing gaze, my focus drops to his mouth — way too demurely considering everything we did last night. "Hey."

His hand moves past my elbow, drops to my waist, and inches to the hem of my shirt. "Anywhere you need to be today?" he asks low, fingers slipping under the material and brushing along my hip.

To keep from waking Trenton, since it appears Hayes is working hard to make sure his best friend stays asleep, I simply shake my head against his shoulder in response.

Since the outfit I wore last night conveniently lacked underwear and Trenton refused to let me wear his shorts to bed, my lower half is completely bare; when Hayes's touch fiddles and seeks, it is all skin on skin.

Every inch of my body, both inside and out, sparks to life — goosebumps rise, nipples perk, core tightens.

Hayes had set his glasses aside last night, leaving no barrier between his dark-blue eyes and mine as our gazes lock. When his exploration leads over my outer thigh to between my legs, my hips immediately curve inward, seeking more.

Once his fingers reach their destination, they slip through easily. He raises an eyebrow and, with a chuckle, asks under his breath, "Do you wake up this wet every morning?"

"Guess we'll have to do some research." I match his breathy tone and give a sly grin. "Something tells me it has to do with who I woke up next to… and how expertly I'm being touched."

His eyelids drop to half-mast, gaze falling to my mouth as his finger dips inside me once and exits slowly. On an unspoken mission, he removes his hand from beneath the covers, raises it up toward my face, and drags the damp pads of his fingers along my bottom lip, wordlessly asking permission to give me a taste of what he had conjured.

I snake my tongue out, and he slips two fingers into my mouth, twisting them in a slow circle before dragging them back out with a quiet groan.

He scrunches his neck down and gives me a soft kiss before moving toward my ear and whispering even lower, "How about you wake Trenton up so he can join us for the morning-after breakfast this time?" His fingers continue tracing the shape of my lips as though he's reliving and memorizing everything about them.

The warm breath accosting my skin causes the length of my neck to tingle. As I shift to my other side, his fingers move to my nape and tangle in the mess of hair there before splaying upward through the strands until his palm is resting loosely on top of my head with the barest of pressure.

I allow him to direct me downward toward a soft, and very-much-still-sleeping, Trenton. As soon as my face is positioned just right, the pressure on top of my head decreases.

So as not to jar Trenton too much and ruin the element of surprise, instead of wiggling his boxers down, I take advantage of that convenient front opening by slipping my finger inside and directing him free.

Amused that the whispering, the slight bounce of the bed with each movement, and the touching still isn't enough to drag him out of the depths of sleep, I press my lips together to control the laugh trying to break loose.

Trenton sleeps hard. Alas, his cock does not, so that will need to be remedied in order for this plan to work. The gentle press against my head proves Hayes agrees.

Since Trenton needs all the help he can get right now, I hold him between my fingers and descend. Consuming his cock completely is easy in this present state, so I take full advantage, pressing my lips all the way against the base.

Hayes lets me continue the wake-up call with full control, simply resting his hand and letting it rise and fall naturally with the slow up and down of my efforts.

It doesn't take long for Trenton's size and shape to begin filling out — his subconscious mind and body reacting to the cues before he is fully alert.

The ever-so-slight drag of my teeth along his length seems to do the trick, though. "Mmm," his groggy voice mumbles. "Hayes… I swear to god… if that's your mouth on my cock when my eyes open, I'm keying your car."

This time I can't hold the laugh in any longer. My lyrical amusement hums around his girth as I peer up from under my lashes.

At first sight, his eyes are still closed. But before long, one peeks open. When he sees me rather than Hayes, his other eye joins in to assess the scene.

He flashes me a quick wink before biting down on his bottom lip with a groan, tracing a finger across my forehead, and tucking a curtain of hair behind my ear.

Locking eyes with Hayes this time, I press my tongue against the bottom of Trenton's cock and swipe upward.

Hayes had somehow managed to reach the bedside table and put his glasses back on while I was busy with Trenton.

Damn.

With that messy hair and glasses-rimmed, lust-glossed gaze, watching him observe me is fire.

I loop my tongue around the tip and open wide to consume Trenton again. Hayes pitches in this time. Fingers clenched in my hair and tongue snaking out to wet his lips, he guides me down.

My focus falls as I take a much firmer, much longer Trenton in and move my head into a small twist around him. Hayes presses against me harder, testing my limits until my eyes water and body reacts with a heave.

Hayes appears to know just how aggressively Trenton prefers to be serviced, and he is determined to make sure it happens. Trenton grunts and lifts his hips, eyes rolling up toward the ceiling.

The mattress dips beside my supporting hand, and I slide back up, returning my alternating attention to each man. Hayes's hand leaves my head as he knee-walks toward the bottom edge of the bed.

The crinkle of a condom wrapper meets my ears, and Trenton palms each side of my face. His gaze leaves the ceiling and falls hooded and heavy on me. He brushes his thumbs along my jaw and to the corners of my filled mouth.

Hayes pushes up my borrowed shirt until the material is above my hips and my ass is on full display. He then lifts me to direct my body into a hands and knees position.

Once situated, his warm fingers move between my legs and through my folds. His motions are slow and cautious. Since he can't gauge my reactions, other than the fact that I'm not pulling away, he somehow gets Trenton's attention to communicate with him instead. Sepia eyes adjust over and past me to meet Hayes's silent directive.

The two of them engage in a wordless conversation for a moment before those light-brown eyes drop to mine in silent inquiry, as if to ask how willing I am — just what, exactly, Hayes is allowed to use that easily-collected lubrication for.

I smile around his cock and take him deep and slow, never unlocking our gazes despite the difficult angle. Trenton bites down on his bottom lip and shakes his head in equal parts amusement and unabridged excitement. With his gaze back on Hayes, they continue their voiceless exchange.

Hayes immediately responds to whatever the conclusion was, fingers dipping inside me again and back up to lubricate every single area he intends to use.

Which, from what I can tell from his ministrations, is all of me — each passage bared to him right now.

And I am more than eager and ready.

Their practiced silent communication adds a whole new dynamic to these experiences with them. As much as I love dirty talk and chesty groans of pleasure, this intimate pantomime makes my mind reel and body churn in unexpected, euphoric ways.

Every part of us — our minds, bodies, and hearts — are completely in tune and ready to perform.

Hayes still doesn't jump to any advanced conclusions just yet, though. Each dive of his fingers, each squeeze of his hand, is deliberate and patient.

Until I press my ass hard against him because of my own impatience — if the maddening, ever-increasing pulse between my legs is any indicator.

Hayes chuckles behind me, but he responds to my eager request in the way he sees most fitting: his cock coasts once through my folds before immersing inside me with a slow inward and upward drive that grazes against every perfect spot.

A whimper blends with the twisting of my tongue up and over Trenton's shaft.

"Ah, damn." Trenton exhales a slow, controlled breath from his lungs. "Seeing you take him while those lips are wrapped around my co—" I plunge downward, earning a grunt of interruption in return.

Hayes and I create a rhythm; when he drives inside me, I deep throat all of Trenton. Trenton tries to add some words into the mix, but with the increasing of his breaths and my attention, talking gets more and more complicated.

When his cock tenses and twitches against the roof of my mouth and his hands move from my head to my shoulders — immediately followed by the light flutter of his fingers tapping against my skin — I pause. Hayes does, too.

Another wordless cue — one I am not well versed in, unfortunately.

My eyes probe Trenton, eyebrows curving inward slightly.

He blows a quiet raspberry from his lips, grimaces, and reveals the reason for the flutter of his fingers against my skin: "Making a guy tap out too soon. I see how it is. You play dirty." His voice drops an octave. "But, damn, I can't get enough."

I love how, even in the throes of sex, Trenton can make me laugh. In the moment, the lust and laughter is an oddly harrowing combination. I'm completely comfortable between them. Then he has to go and make me laugh, sending me into a tailspin of unfair feelings.

My eyes drop to the string ring, and air lodges in my throat. To bypass the poorly-timed flood of girly emotion, I slowly descend over his cock again, choosing to replace the lodged air with something more tangible. Something I can control.

Hayes bends over me. "You know our rule; we finish after you." He reaches around, rubs my clit, and slams inside me. Goosebumps rise everywhere all at once.

Trenton's fingers dig into my shoulder, and he glowers at his best friend. Hayes straightens, but his cock and fingers continue stroking and playing despite the glare of warning.

I do my best to continue working Trenton, but Hayes revs me up too much, his movements increasing speed in practiced, perfect intervals. The overwhelming combination of sensations pull me deep into a thoughtless headspace, nearly rendering me useless.

Reading my body just as well as he reads Trenton, his other hand swaps from where he'd been gripping my hip to my clit, and the hand that had previously been stroking me drags to between my cheeks.

Cock buried inside me and one finger against my clit, his opposite finger makes a statement of its own with an inquisitive, gentle pressure against my only remaining available entrance.

My body caves and melts all at once, curving into him yet feeling as though most all functionality is lost at the same time. Hayes's finger enters me, and I moan around Trenton, unable to function enough to move over him any longer.

His hands return to my head to assist, and he presses downward. I open wide for him while my body concurrently clenches around everywhere Hayes has filled me. Trenton sucks in a breath as I meet his base, my body so supple and yielding that even my gag reflex has all but disappeared. He gently encourages my head back up to the tip, but only for a second before pressing me down over his length once more.

Hayes twists his finger and grinds his hips, and I tighten around him again. Trenton removes one hand from my head and uses his thumb and forefinger to circle the base of his cock, drawing himself down tight and increasing his swell.

As close as I am to a release, I still disagree with their "you before us" rule. Especially when, like last night, we're so in tune as a group; I don't see any reason we can't finish at the same time.

Willing my head and mouth to work just long enough to milk Trenton of everything he has, I suction onto him and increase the speed of my efforts.

As both expected and hoped, the hand that had been directing my head moves toward my shoulder to signal for Hayes to stop. Or else.

But when he does this, I press my ass harder against Hayes. The aggressive entry of both his finger and his cock combined with the swivel of his finger and the swell of Trenton inside my mouth pushes my body over the edge, falling into the abyss of release. As I wail over Trenton's cock, his hand grips my head again, and his hips thrust upward as he joins Hayes and me in an unavoidable, collective release.

Warm fluid coats my throat and Trenton's fingers clench in my hair as he lets out a deep growl. A shudder pulsates inside me as Hayes lets out a chesty grunt.

Completely and suddenly replete, the three of us don't move for several heartbeats — our heavy breathing and quiet buzz of electronics the only sounds in the room.

CHAPTER THREE

Instead of getting dressed in the room, I collect all my clothes and head to the bathroom this time. Getting dressed for the day and a quick brush of my teeth with my finger takes hardly any time. I find myself in there for a long while afterward anyway, staring at seemingly random numbers on a small, golden-colored piece of paper.

Hayes had explained that the numbers equate to a date, time, and location of an upcoming meet — not just a handful of crew members getting together to shoot the shit, but an actual race night, I guess.

If it warrants a special code process, I also presume this meet must be a big deal.

Since the moment they came into my life, I have seesawed between hoping these guys were my way into the very club I was looking for and, as unexpected feelings blossomed and relationships formed, hoping they had nothing to do with the eventual crew my "job" would throw under the bus.

Because with the information, my next step is delivering details of their involvement to my "bosses."

Why?

Why did it have to be them after all?

Dammit.

Perhaps the coincidence wouldn't be so bad if this club that Crow, Trenton, and Hayes manage stands a chance against Jude Delancey and Porter Davis.

But that isn't the case; Revelry will get their asses handed to them on a shiny, chrome platter.

Before, I simply needed a solid lead. Now, I find myself in an unfair position. One that will ultimately demand a choice that I have absolutely no desire to make.

With a growl of frustration, I shove the ticket back into my pocket and exit the bathroom to join Trenton and Hayes in the kitchen for the promised morning-after breakfast.

As soon as I walk in, Trenton charges like a bull, scoops me up, slings me over his shoulder, tromps into the living room, and drops me onto the couch. My hands immediately clutch my chest as I work overtime to reclaim the breaths he had stolen, in more ways than one.

Now hovering over me, fists squished into the couch at each side of my head, he performs a push-up style kiss; mouth, chest, hips — all of him pressing against all of me.

Trenton pushes away and reaches out toward me. I accept, and he pulls me up to a sitting position just as Hayes rounds the side of the couch, carrying two mugs. The scent of freshly ground and brewed coffee swirls around us.

Trenton holds his hand out in Hayes's direction, but Hayes jerks the mug away from him. "You don't even drink coffee. Get something yourself."

"I've changed my mind," Trenton says.

Hayes's eyebrows flatten. Trenton's eyebrows rise. Hayes relents and passes him what was meant to be his personal coffee. He then sits beside me, thigh flush against mine, and delivers my mug.

I dip my nose inside and inhale the toasty scent before taking a sip. "Thank you."

Trenton sits on the coffee table directly across from me, slipping his leg between mine and scooting his butt to the edge so his knee grazes against the apex of my thighs.

He lifts the hot drink to his mouth, waggling his eyebrows at me over the rim. Then his face contorts and tongue wags out in disgust.

Hayes takes the opportunity to steal back his coffee with a laugh.

"Yeah, still don't know how the majority of the population drinks that stuff." Now free of the mug, Trenton places each hand on my thighs and slides his palms upward. I lean back and open my legs a little more. The motion doubles to make my contact with Hayes firmer.

We sit like this for a while in comfortable silence — Hayes and I drinking our coffees, Trenton resting his forearms on the tops of his thighs, head hung down in thought as his fingers draw circles on my skin.

"Hayes and I want—" Whatever Trenton was going to say is interrupted by the opening of the front door. We all turn our attention toward the sound.

Crow enters, kicking the door wider with the tip of his boot, arms full. Once he is across the threshold and the door is shut, his eyes finally take in the scene and immediately find me in the middle of Trenton and Hayes. Those thick, black lashes flutter a few extra times as he blinks repeatedly.

Was he expecting me to be gone already? To have ditched his best friends and gone running back to Porter?

His gaze leaves mine, and he hyper-focuses on the task of dumping everything in his arms onto the dining room table. "Grub… for anyone who wants some."

Seeing as he carried in a few bags of said grub, I imagine he wasn't banking on them turning the offer down. Trenton and Hayes stand. I push myself off the fluffy couch and follow them to the table. Crow's gaze lifts at my approach. "I bought extra if you want some too."

Ah… so I was right. Since my bike is parked in the garage and he entered through the front, he didn't realize I was still here.

How does he feel about that discovery, though?

Had he hoped I would leave before he got back?

"I don't usually eat much for breakfast, but it smells really good," I answer.

His attention flicks past me toward the kitchen then back down at the bags of food. The corner of his lips twitches as he starts taking out individually wrapped sandwiches. I peer over my shoulder in an attempt to figure out what he saw that left him so smug.

The clock. Having been distracted immediately upon exiting the bathroom, I hadn't even caught a glimpse of the time. Morning is well past. He brought lunch… not breakfast.

I grimace, unable to control my reaction. That tick of a smile broadens, and he shakes his head, tossing me a burger without warning.

Wasting no time, I pull out a chair, sit, and open the paper package. Because, damn… It appears I am hungry after all. Probably something to do with the fact that I've been fucked to a famish.

Trenton and Hayes behave similarly, snatching their own burgers without prevail.

Crow joins a bit slower, sitting across from me and emptying the last bag.

When he scoots in his chair, his knee bumps me. But when I wiggle away to give him more room, his chrome eyes lock to my brown ones, and he leans back in the chair, ensuring his knee meets mine again under the table.

He takes a bite, and his tongue snakes out to collect a small piece of bun that had stuck to his labret piercing. In an attempt not to stare, my eyes drop a few inches, landing on the inked fingers gripping the burger. Again, the permanently-etched numbers beg me to open the topic. But yet again, I hold my tongue. Whatever they stand for happened not too long ago. If the tattoo gun was a means for healing an inner wound, that wound might still be raw.

I place my burger on the table, swapping it for my cup of coffee. Now a bit caffeinated and a smidgen fed, I lift my gaze back up to his and push my mug across the table with the tips of my fingers. Then for some absurd reason I say, "Want some 'caw'fee?" stressing the 'caw' in light of his nickname.

Trenton and Hayes had been immersed in some sort of discussion, but their voices were nothing more than distant mumbles as Crow and I engaged in a wordless conversation of our own. Even so, they hear my quip and the room grows quiet for all of two seconds before it fills with boisterous laughter.

Crow, however, isn't as amused. His steely eyes narrow as he tears off another bite. "Cute," he says around a mouthful. His face hardens just as much as the piercing of his eyes does. In contradiction, his knee grazes lightly — intentionally — against mine.

The laughter around the table subsides, but being lost in each other remains. He wraps those tattooed fingers through the handle and brings it to his mouth with a raised eyebrow before returning the mug to between us.

CHAPTER FOUR

When everyone is done eating, none of us make a motion to get up or strike conversation; we're all perfectly content just sitting here in silence and allowing our food to digest.

Crow occasionally brushes my knee with his. My body sparks at the contact every time. Those sparks then travel from my knee up the inside of my thigh before settling hot and low inside me.

Part of me wonders if everyone is so quiet because Crow joined in last night, especially when it was explained beforehand that group intimacy isn't really his thing.

That, and the undeniable friction that fills whatever space in which we find ourselves together.

Eventually, though, Trenton speaks up and cuts through the tension. "So, what does everyone have planned today?" He slouches in his chair. "I have to be at work by four."

Both Hayes and Crow turn their attention to Trenton, and he shrugs away their apparent hesitation.

Since they don't seem overly eager to share their schedules, I pipe up. "Well, I just want to make sure I'm home at some point to check in with Jude… and get an update on Porter."

Crow's jaw moves over clenched teeth as he darts another shady glance at Hayes.

And just like that, the tension in the room skyrockets again. A different type of tension this time, though — thick and angsty.

What happened with Porter last night put a bad taste in all our mouths. I get it. But before and after, we otherwise had a lot of fun together. Even if Crow isn't keen on admitting that, perhaps, he had a good time too. I sure know he enjoyed coming all over my chest.

What happened immediately after Crow left the room — finding the ticket in my shorts — flashes through my mind, and the piece of paper becomes leaden in my pocket.

Seeing as Trenton's casual attempt at conversation isn't going over well, I dig inside my shorts, pull out the paper, and slide it across the table toward Crow, stopping midway beside the coffee.

"Want to tell me more about this?" I ask.

Crow's focus had followed my every motion, from my hand disappearing under the table until it lifted to reveal the piece of paper. Gaze locking with mine, his tongue slips out to toy with his piercing before humoring me with an answer.

Instead of giving me one, though, he turns toward Hayes and raises an eyebrow.

Trenton darts alternating glances between the two men, clearly not abreast of whatever Crow and Hayes are speechlessly conveying.

Since Hayes is directly beside me, the tapping of his fingers on the top of his thigh catches in my peripheral.

His eyes dig into Crow's for a heartbeat before he turns toward me. "My job is manning the financials and organizing the specifics for The Gulf Coasters' meets. Since we have one coming up, that's what I'll be doing over the next few days."

"Your job? As in your source of income?" I realize how nonchalantly I pressed for more details on his financial situation, so I wave a hand, dismissing my own question. "Feel free to plead the fifth."

Hayes gives me a warm smile. "All good. Yeah… well… *unofficially* my source of income." The quick flicker of a glance at both Crow and Trenton does not escape my notice.

They've apparently decided to open up and share some of the more private details with me about this street racing club, but their unease is quite evident.

They know I have some street knowledge. Jude and Porter were the ones enmeshed in the racing scene growing up, though, not me. Dad was never a huge fan. However, if it could somehow bring income into Lance Industries, he would turn a blind eye. Their involvement only extended to the occasional cash event. A mix of gambling with the tease of a weighty chunk of money at the end was enough to keep them active in the scene most weekends if business with Dad wasn't pressing.

But how much knowledge do I share with Crow, Hayes, and Trenton? Within the club Jude and Porter were a part of, the influx of cash was not nearly big enough to act as a supportive income for anyone involved. Sure, a highly sought after grudge match might have resulted in a decent payout on any given cash event, but it was not sustainable for any one person. The pay fluctuated too much, depending on a win was too risky.

"So, are all three of you involved in the management of this club?" I ask.

Trenton, still unsure of what is going on, finally speaks up. "Yep. I head the public relations department."

Hayes laughs and leans back in his chair, much more comfortable now that Trenton has become involved.

I press my lips together and leer at Trenton.

He gives me a wink and says, "In short, I handle the recruiting and pass out the tickets. What with my killer personality and all."

"Now that last part, I believe."

He flashes me a grin, and I turn my attention on Crow. "CEO," he answers in short.

"Oh… fancy," I respond while taking a turn at this little game of touch we've been playing under the table.

Heh. Under the table. A lot like this group they manage and the apparent money involved.

"Do you have a job outside of the club?" I dare ask Crow.

He props his elbows up on the table, temples his fingers at his mouth, and shakes his head, fingers rubbing against his bottom lip.

Well, damn. If these guys can live off the income they make through the club, that certainly explains why Jude and Porter are so interested. Moreso, why they won't just start from scratch to form their own. If there is already an established and effective monetary system in place, it makes sense they would want to cut that corner — overtake what is already organized. Steal the blood, sweat, and tears it took to get The Gulf Coasters the apparent prestige it has today.

I love my brother and father. More than anything. But Dad was never flowers and rainbows in his dealings. Neither is Jude. As sweet as my brother can be, he's ruthless like Dad. Possibly worse.

Jude's methods are just smoother than how Porter approaches business. Good cop, bad cop type of thing. At least with Porter, you know what to expect — vileness all around. Jude is a human nitrous system — runs pretty stock until the right button is pushed.

The guys are quiet as they wait for me to continue the conversation, giving me an illusion of control. In reality, it is a tactic I know well — a way of doing their own assessment, based on my response. Or lack thereof. Clearing the shock from my throat, I ask Crow, "If Trenton is head of PR, why were you the one to give me the ticket?"

Again, his jaw moves over clenched teeth, and that damn stifling tension smothers the room.

Just when I think he's not going to give me an answer, he says, "Figured with the way you handled your bike last night, you might be interested." He shrugs a shoulder, reaches forward, slides the ticket back toward me, then lifts the mug of our shared coffee to his mouth.

I reaccept the ticket, giving the details one more thorough study before returning it to my pocket. "Sounds like a good time." Unable to hold his penetrative gaze, my focus drops to the ochre-colored ring of spilled coffee marking the resting spot of our mug. "Consider it penciled in," I whisper, unwilling to make any promised commitment. Pencil marks can be erased after all.

He nods, slams the mug down onto the table, and stands. "Right. Well, my girl needs a bit of maintenance, so I'm gonna get her lubed up. You kids have fun." He snatches his key off the bar top, and salutes us all en route to the door.

I shoot to my feet, dashing a glance at Trenton and Hayes. "Hey…. Umm… I need to head out, too. Okay?"

Both Hayes and Trenton push out of their seats and straighten. The scene becomes incredibly awkward as we all look at each other, Crow in position to twist the doorknob but frozen on the spot.

"Don't leave yet," I squeak, hating how desperate the plea sounds. "Let me just make sure I have everything I came here with, and I'll be right out."

Crow nods and grunts, opening the door and exiting before I can say anything else and sound even more pathetic than I already do.

Thoroughly embarrassed, I don't bother looking at Hayes or Trenton as I spin around and grab my fob off the bar top.

They have other plans, though. Plans that don't include me walking out the door without an intervention first.

Hayes approaches, one hand shoved in a pocket, the other hanging loosely at his side. When we're face to face, the hand at his side lifts and rubs the back of his neck. "Trenton and I want you to put together a weekend bag. One that you can keep here."

I glance over his shoulder and peer at Trenton as he leans against the table, palms pressed along the edge on either side of his hips as though ready to propel forward should I try to escape. He gives me a crooked grin, and all my budding anxiousness dissipates.

When my attention returns to Hayes, he continues. "We're not asking you to move in" — he lets out a nervous chuckle — "but, we definitely want to see more of you and figured you might eventually get tired of wearing borrowed or dirty clothes every time you come over."

My hands come to the hem of the shorts I've been wearing on and off for the past twenty-four-plus hours.

Trenton pushes off the table and approaches Hayes's side. "Plus, that way you don't have to wear a backpack while riding on your bike every time you come over. Just leave the bag here, and we'll take care of the rest — make sure your clothes stay clean, things like that."

Damn. These men plead a good case. I know what they're not saying, though; they want me staying away from Porter as much as possible. But staying away from Porter means also staying away from Jude, and I'm not sure I can handle that yet. Not when wounds are still so raw and we are both still suffering and dependent on each other to get through our grief.

"Wow, you have rendered me speechless. First the ring, now the keys. Next thing you'll expect is for me to drop my pants before we're married. Sorry, boys; I'm just not that type of girl."

Hayes's lips quirk upward and he tilts his head down to look up at me over the rim of his glasses. "Well, if what happened last night and this morning is your version of not being that type of girl, you just keep on that trend."

Trenton winks at me, steps forward, loops his arm around my lower back, and pulls me in close. "Meet me at the courthouse. I can't fucking wait to see what type of girl you become after the commitment is official."

Hayes slaps him on the shoulder. "Keep it up T-Top, and you'll scare her off."

A wide grin spreads across my face as Trenton presses his nose and forehead against mine while stiff arming Hayes in the chest. Hayes stumbles backward, hand coming up to rub the spot of impact.

The rumble of Crow's car sparking to life has me jerking in Trenton's hold and stealing a glance at the door. Trenton lets go, and I step around him.

Just as I'm turning the doorknob, a hand wraps around mine, and my attention moves to the culprit — Hayes this time. My hand drops from the knob as he takes a turn drawing me toward him for a quick kiss.

"I liked waking up with you this morning. Don't make it the last time," he says.

My knees turn weak and pulse revs. I swallow hard and give him a curt nod. His fingers drag across my hip and continue on past me. The door then creaks open, and he ushers me out.

CHAPTER FIVE

Trenton

T he door clicks closed, but Hayes continues to stare at the spot where Remi just stood.

Hayes and I had a lot of fun last night and this morning, but we don't get hung up on girls. We don't stop them before they leave and ask them to come back. We don't miss them when they're gone.

Watching Hayes react the way I feel makes my stomach churn. I brought her into his room, opening the proverbial door that let him know I was good with sharing. As usual.

Had I expected him to simply be okay with just a little between-the-sheets activity and nothing more?

Yeah… maybe.

The women we bring into our beds are typically not something we need to 'discuss' either. There's no before and after planning. One of us brings one home — which is usually me — if she's down, we're down. But this is about to turn into a conversation. For sure.

And something tells me the reason he still hasn't turned around is no longer because he still smells her and feels the linger of her goodbye kiss, but because I'm behind him. When he leaves the door, he has to face how he feels — how we both feel.

I return to my leaning spot against the table and wait, watching him go through the nervous ticks that I've memorized over the years: The tapping of his fingers on the side of his thigh; The rubbing of the back of his neck.

I wait for the final one. The one where he lifts his hand to push his glasses up the bridge of his nose before being ready to address what he's struggling to come to terms with.

The motion comes, and he turns around, his posture straight. He knew I'd been watching him, so my presence isn't a surprise. But I can tell by the slightly inward curve of his shoulders that he was hoping I'd disappeared into my room.

For too long, we stare at each other, trying to figure out how to start the conversation. Or, rather, decide which topic to discuss first.

A small smile ticks up on his face, and he lifts a finger, pointing it in my direction. "I blame you."

I laugh. Crow, Hayes, and I always enjoy seeking out opportunities to place blame, especially where it's due. It's usually in a lighthearted way, so points to Hayes for using our friendly game to cut through the awkward tension. At least he didn't go straight into denial mode; that's more along the lines of Crow's modus operandi.

His hand scoops around the back of his neck again, and he shifts from foot to foot. "So, uh… I guess we need to talk?"

"Yeah." I cross my arms over my chest, barricading my fucking heart.

He nods slowly, drops his hand back to his side, and takes a seat at the table behind me. I turn around and follow suit, plopping into the seat across from him.

Knowing him the way I do, I attempt to strategically lead the oncoming conversation — by order of importance. I know we can both agree making sure Remi stays safe is at the top. "Think she'll take us up on our offer?" I ask.

He reclines, lifts his glasses with one hand, pinches the bridge of his nose with the other, and shakes his head. "No. Not right away at least. It's not that simple. She'll go back to him. They always do.

She's not scared enough, yet. Best we can do right now is keep her busy. The more she's with us, the less she's with him."

That line Hayes is referring to, between feeling enough fear to get the hell away from the situation versus the moment it's too late and something terrible happens, is paper-cut fine.

The water on the table that I had opted for earlier begins gyrating in the glass, moving in erratic swooshes back and forth as Hayes bounces his knee. "I know" — he lets out a breath — "I know I'm not the type to lay someone out. But I will." His eyes burn red to the point where he has to remove his glasses and place them on the table.

Fuck.

I lean forward, hands clasped between us. "I know, man. You'd fucking lay him out." My own eyes burn. Fuck, fuck, fuck.

I can count on one hand the number of times throughout the years Hayes and I have known each other that we've come this close to his past resurfacing. Our pasts. It stings. A burn smolders in my heart.

I don't want him to say it, but I know he will. It's been too long. And we both know if he doesn't talk it out, he'll spiral. The best thing I can do for him right now is wait and listen.

The waiting doesn't take long; he's eager to get it over with. "I couldn't help her. I was too fucking weak and lanky and shit." His hands fist and drop to the table, landing with a thud. "I was her only hope... and... and I could hardly defend myself against him much less protect her. If I could fucking rewind time, there are so many things I would change. If I had just done something... anything... she could still be alive."

I want to spout the typical, "It's not your fault," bullshit, because it's not his fucking fault. But who really wants to hear that when grieving? No goddamn one, that's who.

"I know, man. Instead of in the slammer, he'd be in the dirt."

Hayes nods resolutely. He has never been the brawny type. Never. But that doesn't stop him from working out every day just to prove design wrong. In doing so, he had turned his weakness into strength.

He's my biggest damn idol, and it breaks my heart seeing him this way.

If there's a lifeline to be thrown at Remi, he will cast it. Every time. And, yeah, it might have started out as somewhat of a charity case — him seeing a broken girl and driven by his past to fix her — but that charity blazed into a flame really fast. This has nothing to do with charity now and everything to do with the fact he is starting to care about her.

With a deep breath, he locks away the memory of his dad abusing his mother to death and takes the conversation on the most obvious natural course. "Thanks for including me last night," he says.

"Thanks for the head this morning, bro." I give him a wink and he laughs, swiping at his eyes one more time before putting his glasses back on.

Silence descends between us again, but our eyes meet, both of us willing and ready for the conversation at hand.

The irony is that we don't know what to say. How do you even start a conversation like this? *Hey, bro, you can have her even though she runs through my fucking thoughts every second of every day?*

Heh. Right.

Instead, I state the obvious: "Sharing has never steered us wrong in the past; why should it now?"

His knee stops bouncing, the water in the glass stills, and his hands slide off the table and land in his lap where I assume he has begun tapping a steady pattern.

"Tell me how you really feel," he prods.

I rest back in the chair, distancing myself just in case this goes bad. "Like I want the girl and my best friend, too," I respond with a whisper.

His eyes bore into mine. "Yeah… same here."

That is enough for me. There's no need to sit here and drift around the topic. So, I straighten in my chair and press into the next one. "Do you know anything about her brother?"

Hayes straightens, too, the spark of challenge lighting in his eyes. "No, but I think it's time to do a little digging."

CHAPTER SIX

Remi

Crow's patience had waned while Trenton and Hayes were saying their goodbyes. My heart does a stupid little jump at finding him still waiting on me anyway. He sits in his car with the windows rolled down, head back against the headrest, eyes closed, and wrist draped over the top of the steering wheel.

I approach the passenger side and dip my head down. Just as I am about to clear my throat to get his attention, one of his eyes peeks open, and he turns his head toward me.

He doesn't bother to indicate whether or not I should come around to the driver's side to talk to him. And he certainly doesn't go out of his way to get out. Unwilling to keep hunched over to speak with him through the passenger window, I make a bold decision. Before I can overthink the potential consequences, I open the door and slip in. As soon as I'm safely tucked inside, Crow puts the car into gear and drives us away.

I rush to buckle in, but he darts a sideways glance at me and says, "Don't bother; we're just going down to the end of this side road right here."

I imagine he would point ahead if it weren't for the fact that we're already there and he's making the turn. The belt slips through my fingers and falls back to the seat behind my shoulder as his tires jostle over a different section of the train track I remember crossing en route to Hayes and Trenton's house.

As seems typical for Crow and me at this point, we both keep quiet as he drives down the length of the backroad. By the time we're at the end, the train track and road have converged again.

He pulls into a field that is closed off to the main roads. The track runs through to our left, parallel to the main road that runs behind the house, but there's a barricade of woods between the two, creating an empty oasis of trees and railway.

He loops around and backs up so the trunk of his car is facing the track, then he gets out and I quickly follow suit.

I simply want to thank him for the intervention last night — apologize for riding recklessly and making him have a panic attack — in gentler words, of course. It's not my intention to dawdle or make this complicated.

Crow leans against his bumper and looks up at me before darting a glance to the spot next to him.

Overcome by an unexpected nervousness, I hesitate. Nervous because even a few paces away from each other the air vibrates between us. I might very nearly be crushed by the pressure if I sit next to him.

He's not the type to care about my decision either way, though. When I don't sit right away, he shrugs it off and shoves his hands in his pockets, staring ahead at the track.

After a mental battle of wills, lasting probably all of five seconds yet feels like an hour, I prop against the bumper, fingers curving around the shape, ready for assistance launching away should the need arise.

Crow's posture is much more relaxed than mine.

Maybe that always-present, heady tension is only one-sided. Maybe his shoulder doesn't ache at the point where our bodies are closest. For some wild reason, my brain-to-mouth filter stops working completely at the recognition, and a breathless, "Do you feel that?" comes out. The thought had originally been meant for me and me alone, but my voice had other plans.

The comment seems stilted falling off my tongue. Like there's more. An explanation. Out of context, what I asked surely doesn't make sense. And since the context was mental, but the comment verbal, I don't dare steal a glance over at him and witness the look he gives me when piecing together that I might be just slightly insane. Around him at least.

However, his response comes nearly as fast as my question. "Yep."

That single word floats heavy between us. The tension in my neck and shoulders loosens, but all the tension elsewhere heightens, making my body a mashup of confusion.

"I… I wanted to say thank you. For being at the pier last night. For stepping in."

"No need to thank me. I was there because I don't trust you," he explains. "I would have done the same thing for a complete stranger."

My teeth clack together between pressed lips, but I accept his response. "How about coming on my chest last night? That something you do for strangers, too?" I straighten, but the change in posture and my remark is purely a facade; Crow's words stung, and guilt pumps through my veins. He's smart not to trust me.

What's worse, though, is that I want his trust. *Their* trust. But seeing as there's a harrowing division of my heart and mind at the present, hell... I don't trust myself.

Now it's his turn to grind his teeth at the accusation. Crow's head slowly bobs up and down, but not in response; it's more as an acceptance of the volley.

We both know the answer to my question. Trenton and Hayes had already explained that his participation last night was out of character. He'd already told me once that group stuff wasn't his thing.

So... Why?

Why was last night any different?

I certainly hadn't given him reason to want me. This thing between us has been undesired at the best of moments, dreaded at the worst. But the strange connection drew him into the room last night. Had he not come inside, it would have somehow convinced me to seek him out at some point.

I study him since he refuses to look at me. The imprint of his fingers curl in the tightly drawn black material of his jean pockets.

"Anyway… I just wanted to thank you, and apologize if I overstepped in some way. The streets run through my veins just as much, if not more, than they run in yours. I might be a woman, but just like Hayes wasn't going to sit on the sidelines last night despite it having nothing to do with him, I wasn't going to sit aside as a damsel in distress and let someone else take the fall on my behalf."

Crow rounds on me then, hands immediately popping free from the cage of his pockets so he can point a finger in my face. "See" — that same finger waggles in front of my nose — "Trenton and Hayes are tossing you a buoy due to a situation you refuse to admit is toxic, and you still continue risking your life all for the sake of pride."

My eyebrows lift but quickly fall into a flat line as I swat his hand out of my face.

He cocks his head at me and scoffs. "Oh, so you'll defend yourself against me, but not against Porter? And don't feed me that 'you don't understand, our situation is different' bullshit. Those are victim words."

Ohh I hate him so much right now. I want to scream the exact words he'd just told me not to say, clench my hands at my sides, and go into straight tantrum-mode. Because the situation with Porter *is* different... and he *doesn't* understand. "No, I defended myself against you because you aren't a threat. I am not scared of you, Crow."

Crow steps forward, takes my face in his palms, and pierces me with those chrome eyes. "You should be. And you should be *more* scared of Porter than you are."

Everything other than my head reacts — in the least fearful way. I press my mouth against his. I don't slam it out of rebellion, although I wish that were the case. Instead, the rebellion takes a different approach; there's a strange sweetness delivered. A sweetness that dares him to prove just how afraid of him I should be.

Our breaths mingle with a mix of coffee and unspoken curses. My lips brush against his, upper lip grazing against the piercing I'm always so enthralled by. His fingers dig into the side of my head, and his breathing triples. For a second, I fear he might pass out from the inner conflict as his gaze flicks wildly across mine.

The connection wins, pummeling his rebellion into the ground at our feet. His lips feather against mine, soft and careful — in complete opposition to the bruising press of his fingertips in the hair behind my ears as though his body and mouth are run by two separate brains — or hearts.

His tongue slips in to taste and blend with mine, but their flavors are one in the same: Bitter with a broken past; Sweet with the rebellion of hopeful change; Salty with guilt and regret.

The saltiness wins over, stinging our gaping wounds. The punishment delivered with the tips of our tongues. He pushes away from me with a mumbled curse. "Goddammit." He steps forward again. "You're fucking poison. You said what you wanted to say, now get in the car."

If he thinks he's getting a dumbfounded eye flutter from me, he's wrong. If he thinks any form of hurt is going to flash at him through my dark-brown eyes, he's wrong.

I shrug and chuckle, responding with nothing more than an "Okay," as I push off the bumper and escape his outburst by opening the door and situating myself patiently inside.

Through the passenger side mirror, I watch as he stands and drags his tattooed hand over his face before circling around to the driver's side, opening the door, plopping down, and turning the engine over.

CHAPTER SEVEN

After a good night's rest and plenty of distracting recreation, I had overcome my anxiousness about returning home.

Or so I had thought.

Every mile closer to "home" I get, the more my body is overcome with dread. I'm half tempted to steal away somewhere until my internal, mental problems and all the "what nows" have been figured out.

My worry for Jude overrides everything else, though, so I don't veer off the intended path.

Still, that worry doesn't change my body's response to being forcefully pushed against the current of its wishes: When I park my bike, my knees weaken; When I take the stairs toward the door, my pulse goes into overdrive; When I slide the door open, the blood rushes to my feet.

My heart slams to a stop when I glimpse a figure sitting in the corner of the room in Dad's recliner. When I realize it's Jude, it returns to its steady thump.

In fact, all that dread and nervousness goes away entirely when I surmise that Porter doesn't seem to be around at all. While I noticed his car isn't here, it didn't stop my anxiousness from escalating or my mind from becoming overactive with thoughts of him being home when I arrived.

"You startled me." I give Jude a breathy chuckle. He doesn't say anything at first, just remains reclined in the chair with his elbows propped on the armrests and fingers templed at his mouth.

I deposit my stuff on the bar top, pull a stool away from the island, place it in front of him, and sit. His hands drop, and he gives me a smile. A very tired one. Black circles pool under his glassy eyes. "When was the last time you slept?" I ask.

Jude sighs and rests his head back against the chair. "Last night was the first time you've stayed away since…" he mumbles toward the ceiling, letting the difficult words hang in the air.

Eyebrows knitting inward and voice tremulous, I attempt to allay his concerns. "I would have come home last night if you wanted me to."

Jude straightens, shakes his head, and places a hand on my knee. "Remi, you're a grown woman. The offer was sweet but unnecessary."

Hell, I've been having to remind myself of that a lot lately. Those words paired with the deepened lines around his mouth and eyes are exactly why I keep needing the reminder; Jude has aged what seems like twenty years since Dad passed.

Grief looks different for everyone, and his is thick and festering. Eating away at him slowly, consuming him.

The scariest part is that the job of inheriting Dad's mantle — and taking the Gulf Coast by storm and dredging us out of looming debt — has no room for grief. A grieving person is not always in their right mind. Grief and responsibility? The two can be a dangerous combination.

"Grown woman or not, I have your back, Jude. Let me be your 80 percent if you can only give 20 percent. I know you'd do the same for me." My offer is genuine but coated in shame and regret. If only I could give him 100 percent. But that would mean unearthing dangerous secrets and delving even more into company goings-on.

Neither of which I am prepared to do right now. If ever.

His fingers squeeze over my knee and brown gaze locks with mine. "I visited Porter last night at the hospital. They had him doped up on morphine, but he... He mentioned you."

My stomach and heart clash.

Oh no. That can go so many terrible ways.

What did Porter say?

How can I make it right?

"I'm not Dad..." Jude continues, "but you know you can talk to me, right?"

My lungs seize and vision blurs. God, I want to talk to my brother and best friend more than anything right now.

What if I tell him about Porter and me?

What if I open up about the night Dad died?

Will things get better? Or worse?

Will he stop trusting me altogether?

He is all the family I have.

Pulse thundering in my ears, I open my mouth to reveal something. Anything. But what?

The street racing meet I now finally have information on? Porter's vindictiveness? What happened that night on the port with Dad?

Words get jammed between my mind and mouth, but Crow's comment about being a victim screams loudly in my head. Of the sea of uncertainty in which I am presently entangled, one thing is for certain: I do not want to be a victim. "You should make sure all of Dad's ad- and post-mortem paperwork Porter took care of is in order." What I really want to tell him to do is start seeking out a new Chief Financial Officer.

Jude's black eyelashes flutter. Whatever he'd been hoping or expecting me to reveal, based on what Porter might have said to him in the hospital... I either nailed it or missed the mark completely. Only time will tell.

I have never premeditatedly meddled in work dealings, but the logical side of my brain insists that by stating this particular item of business, I am covering almost every single base of my present issues where family and company are concerned — all four corners of the cell I'd found myself locked in.

In truth, the suggestion is only part logic. A good portion of this recommendation comes from my gut. The answers Jude needs are likely somewhere in plain sight if he digs deep enough. As CEO, he has the resources and talent.

Hell, if only I had given myself that same tip weeks ago; maybe finding a tracker on my bike wouldn't have come as such a damn surprise.

For the first time since this madness started, I'm a little disappointed about my sheltered upbringing when it comes to the family business — upset that I was so adamantly kept out of the loop my whole life. Moreso, I am angry with myself for not caring more. I should have applied myself a little.

Knowledge is power, after all.

And I lack both.

Perhaps it's time for that to change.

I might not fully understand the ins and outs of Lance Industries' dealings and other legal matters, especially the full scope of responsibilities of such positions whether it be that of CEO, CFO, POA — or whatever other mind-boggling acronym — but that doesn't discount the fact that something fishy is going on.

I can easily wrap my mind around how simple it would be for Porter to just say, "Your dad probably has had a tracker on her bike and phone since the day he gave it to her."

A caring, protective father well-versed in the automotive industry? The idea wouldn't be so far-fetched. And, yeah, maybe he did. But what remains to be said is why it's still connected and how coincidental it is that Porter showed up at both the meetup and the pier last night.

Crow was right, and I was obliviously distracted enough — by both responsibility and grief — to not put the possibility of two and two together myself.

That is precisely where the apparent trouble lies. But I am not so certain Jude is ready to hear that his life-long best friend and non-blood brother isn't only screwing his sister but quite possibly his life and business, too, if my increasing assumptions as of late are correct.

Hopefully my simple, roundabout request is enough to nudge Jude in the right direction — take him down a path that will reveal everything I know and maybe even more that we aren't aware of. Things these invisible, binding chains refuse to let me share.

After an uncomfortably long pause, Jude chokes out, "I've been trying to." It isn't this admittance that has his emotions caving inward, though; it's the fact he wasn't at the hospital when Dad was pronounced dead. Jude was states away on a job and couldn't get there fast enough.

And me? Shook up from the events, I was cowering in a dark corner, licking my wounds — waiting for a phone call telling me Dad was okay. Denying what had happened. Falling asleep in an ocean of tears, hoping I would wake up and discover it had been nothing but a nightmare.

When Jude and I finally walked into the hospital together — because lord knows I couldn't do it by myself — we were too late. Dad was gone. According to the attending physician, just prior to his final breaths, Dad had mentioned something about an updated will that would supersede the current one.

After Dad died, Jude turned the house upside down and spent hours going through all the electronic files. Even after entirely clearing out the house to move across the country, there was still no sign of anything different than the will already filed with the courts.

Things had been a whirlwind since then. As Chief Financial Officer of Lance Industries and family friend, Porter was taking care of everything in an effective and efficient manner, remotely nonetheless — a tremendous blessing amid such dour circumstances. Porter picked up the slack where Troy Delancey's children fell short. Our proverbial rock, right?

Since both company and legal matters go right over my head, I left it to the men in my life who know Dad's business like the back of their eyelids.

To hear that Jude is already trying to do the very thing I just suggested tells me something is churning in his gut, too. Jude and I are pragmatic personality types. Anything instinctual comes into play and we generally don't hesitate to follow that trail — such an occurrence being a rarity after all.

Conversation at a stilted, but natural, end for now, Jude stands and stretches, his expressions once again masked.

He extends a hand, I take it, and he pulls me to him, pressing my face against his chest in one of his vulnerable embraces. His chin comes to the top of my head, and he rotates us slowly in a silly twist-hug.

When he steps back, taking my forearms in his hands, he looks at me with a side-grin and says, "We have enough interest to pull off a high-dollar grand opening meet."

His grin widens, and my knees grow weak. After all his hard work — after finally making progress — he's sharing his excitement with the one person who just promised to be his 80 percent. This meet serves as a light at the end of Jude's personal grief-tunnel.

I flash him a forced — but realistic enough — smile.

"Money speaks, Remi. This ought to get us the attention we need to take over the scene. Start low on the totem pole with street racing and move up from there."

"Sounds to me like you don't need my kick-ass sleuthing efforts anymore." I give a half-hearted chuckle, both immensely relieved but also sad that I didn't make him proud.

"Oh, no… I still need you. Porter has been nothing but full of praise about your involvement. The tags you provided him gave us something to follow. Some guys named Burke Halston and Hayes

Collins. We're still tracking the lead, but they're definitely involved and influential."

"T-tags?" Confusion quickly turning to anger, and anger quickly turning to rebellion, I chuckle and wave a hand. "Oh, right. Their license plate numbers. Yeah… no big deal." I throw on another fake, beaming grin. "Hell yeah, bro! Great job. Dad would be proud. This club won't know what hit 'em."

He laughs and gives my arms a squeeze. The short-term happiness in his gaze disappears as his eyes travel over my face.

My pulse judders as his perusal lands on my cheek; the corrective makeup from yesterday has worn off. But he doesn't say anything. His eyes meet mine once more before he steps away and turns toward the stairs. "Now that you're here, I need to grab a few winks. Wake me up if Porter shows?"

A pent up breath flees my lungs. "Yeah. Sweet dreams," I say, finishing with a soft, yet pressed-lipped smile.

CHAPTER EIGHT

As soon as Jude is out of sight, my anger rages. Crow, Hayes, and I may have won the race last night, but Porter still bested us; writing down their license plates was an underhanded move. I knew something was up when Porter so quickly yielded to Crow's demand that he leave. To him, he had won.

And it appears he did.

Come on, Remi.

Why do you seem so surprised yet again?

Unbidden, my feet lead me to the office, and I drop into the chair, flicking into a spin and letting it move round and round until it comes to a stop. Then, I scoot forward and power on the computer.

"Yeah… well… two can play that game," I mutter under my breath as I log into the forum where Revelry handles most of their communications and organizing. "Big mistake bringing me into the fold, Porter. You should've left me out of this."

I have zero desire to screw up what Jude is working on; he has aspirations and shoes to fill after all, and who am I to pull the rug from under him?

I'm his 80 percent, that's who. And as his 80 percent, I think a little meddling would do him some good. A small action for the benefit of all, right?

Mostly, though, Porter needs a wakeup call. Or at least a reminder that being in the company doesn't necessarily mean he has the right to manipulate my family.

Porter wants me to be an infiltrator?

Yeah… I can do that.

After verifying my profile is offline so as not to draw unwanted attention, I scroll the list of members until I see HazerBeam.

Neither of us have come clean about our identities on this forum, yet, and they haven't exactly given me an official invite. But Hayes is smart. He knows; surely he does.

In part, our secretive and playful interactions on here, in between seeing each other in person, have played a big role in bringing us together to the level at which we find ourselves.

If he doesn't realize it's me, then he's a much bigger flirt than I had originally given him credit for.

A small spark of jealousy ignites at the thought that he could be online flirting with other female members in this forum.

Heh, Remi... you're jealous of yourself. How's that for common sense?

:DoubleD: *pew, pew!*

Hayes doesn't respond right away, but when he does, it's with the customary toy gun emoji.

:DoubleD: *Having a good day so far?*

:HazerBeam: *Best morning I've had in a while. Things took a turn for the "okay" just after lunch. You?*

:DoubleD: *Huh. Same.*

Our chat stills, the typing bubbles not popping up on either of our ends. That uncomfortable pause gives my stomach just enough time to churn around the lunch that marked the point of the day said enjoyability changed: when I had left their house.

I have a reason for logging in, though. A plan. Despite the nausea from my nerves trying to get the best of me, I grit my teeth and press my fingers to the keys again:

:DoubleD: Hypothetically, if I were to have some important information for anyone who might be involved in the street racing scene around the area, is it safe to assume the news would get delivered to the right people through you?

It takes me a good minute to work up the courage to click send. The major convincing element is the sense of anonymity this way; my name, my history, my identity is likely just a theory for Hayes.

For me, too; there's always a chance this person isn't Hayes at all. But with his activity in the forum dating back for a few years, right alongside Crow's profile engagement, is plenty evidence that he is, in the least, not someone connected with Jude and Porter. And that's enough proof for the purpose of this plan.

:HazerBeam: I might know a guy who knows a guy.

The little girl in me, the one who kept out of this crap all her life for reasons like the arm wrestle I find myself refereeing now, wants compromise.

Before, I didn't want anything to do with it. Now, I want the details. From both sides. For the purpose of world peace… Even if it means the world is simply a road and the battle is a race between clubs.

There's nothing simple about street wars. Nothing at all. For that reason, what I'm going to do is dangerous, and it'll need to be handled very, very carefully.

:DoubleD: Rumor has it, two different clubs are planning upcoming, large-scale meets.

One sentence. For now, that is all I'm willing to say. Nothing incriminating against Jude. Nothing specific like dates, times, and locations. Hell, I don't even know those details. I'd purposefully refused to look up the map coordinates on the golden ticket. I'd purposefully avoided asking Jude for more information about their planned meet. Sometimes contrived ignorance is the best course of action —

like defense attorneys who tell their clients that they don't want to hear the story. Because the moment they do, their defense is a lie and they become more like an accomplice.

With that one sentence, I manage to share there's a new crew, they're not looking to merge, and money is likely involved.

…and that, damn, I am conflicted. I want to help, but don't really know who or how. Especially while keeping myself free from Porter's wrath.

What the guy on the other end of this conversation chooses to believe or do with the information is up to him and his crew.

Ensuring both crews are aware of each other evens the playing field a little more. The action is not much, but it's a start and at least puts me in a more neutral position. What else to do with that objective placement, however, is yet to be determined.

CHAPTER NINE

"**D**oubleD?" Trenton lifts an eyebrow. "This — woman — has been talking to you on the forum, and you haven't mentioned anything?"

I turn to him and give him the same incredulous look he's trying to give me. "Get a profile, T-Top and maybe you wouldn't be so out of the loop."

"Nah, man. Texting is where I draw the line with that social media shit. You sure that's Remi? She… doesn't have double D's. Not that I'm complaining."

My eyes roll up toward the ceiling.

"What?!" Trenton gasps.

"Good thing you don't have an account after all. She would have lumped you into the category with everyone else that has had something to say about her profile name of choice."

"Well, I mean… just calling it like I see it."

I return my attention to the screen, not bothering to continue this conversation with him face to face. "If you did have a profile, my guess is your name would be T-Top or something along those lines, right?"

"Yeah…"

"Just like everyone else, her name is a play on what she drives — or, rather, rides in her case."

"Doub—ohhh. Ducati Diavel. DoubleD. Huh. Smart. Hang on for a second while I talk my dick down." Trenton clutches himself and throws a crooked grin.

"Yeah, with her? Good luck with that."

"For all you know, this could be some perverted old classics guy hitting on you."

"Check it out for yourself and see what you think." He's not entirely wrong. Sure, DoubleD could be anyone. Shrugging off his comment and crossing my arms, I lean back as he reads our most recent conversation over my shoulder.

"If it's Remi, then Crow was right — she's involved with them somehow," Trenton points out.

"Not somehow. Through Porter, no doubt."

"Right. But see… if she was trying to betray us, she wouldn't have sent this message."

"Betray us? Now you sound like Crow." I swipe a hand through my hair and lean forward again, propping my elbows on the desk. "You two throw that word around as though she's known us for a long time and has reason to *not* betray us. I mean, we haven't exactly been forthcoming either."

"Fair point. Our secrets come with the job, though."

"Right."

Silence hangs between us — that same uncomfortable silence from earlier when we'd just casually decided to share her outside of the bedroom, too. This time, instead of Trenton saying what we're both thinking, I give it a shot: "Pretty sure we are both hopeful that she isn't doing that, though. Betraying us... or the club."

Trenton is quiet for a beat, and his eyes go unfocused. "Yeah," he breathes out, blinking away whatever thought had consumed him for a moment before adjusting his focus to me. A past demon, no doubt; one he'd long ago refused to ever entertain again. "But... why not just tell us about this supposed club straight out? Especially after you and that guy went nose-to-nose? Why the cryptic forum message?"

His question is not unwarranted. I had read and reread this message wondering the same thing — trying to read between the lines. "A call for help is almost always silent," I whisper. "And the ones coming from the smartest, most headstrong victims are always the hardest to decode."

A sense of unease slips down my spine. I pick up my phone and send Remi a text.

:Me: Drinks at The Crowbar tonight? Trenton said he's got a twenty-dollar tab with your name on it.

I flash him the text just so he has a heads up. He nods and claps me on the shoulder. "Let me know what you find. I gotta run."

"Yep." I slide my phone onto the desk and lean back in my chair, rocking it into a steady bounce.

"Cool. Hey, I wouldn't be opposed to having her waiting in my bed when I get home tonight. Make it happen." He flashes me a grin and bounces his eyebrows as he backs out of the room and closes the door behind him.

I immediately lean forward and pick up my phone, hoping I'd somehow missed the vibration of a response.

No response.

Yet, Hayes. Yet.

The mystery surrounding her is a significant reason she has us all so interested. Well, in the beginning it was. Even for Crow, too. He, however, doesn't like mysteries much. Remi is a problem he can't solve.

A large part of that mystery is the fact that we know absolutely nothing about her brother. All I do know is that she seems to care about him. I mean, they're siblings after all. But I saw the way her whole body responded when he told her he loved her. They're close.

So that begs a couple important questions: is he involved in this new crew, too? And, more importantly, why doesn't he know that this guy, Porter, who is living under the same damn roof as him, is roughing up his sister?

Of course, the abuser is often a person in a close relationship with the victim, and they can be very, very good at covering their tracks.

This tells me one of two things: either her brother is involved and is knowingly turning a blind eye, for some reason, or he has absolutely no clue.

I would never in a million years pry into someone's privacy without a damn good reason. Remi's safety is a damn good reason. Who are we dealing with, and who, exactly, do we need to protect her from?

…and do we need to protect ourselves from her?

CHAPTER TEN

Remi

I sign out of the forum, delete the browser history and internet cookies, and return to the living room. As soon as I cross into the hallway, Porter's bulky frame comes into view. He's facing away from me and appears to be focused on something in his hands — head angled down, elbows bent. My feet skid to a halt, and I slowly and quietly begin backpedaling.

I don't escape far enough before he turns around, leans against the bar top, shoves his hands in his pockets, and pierces me with a glare.

That rebellious alter ego of mine has this sick fascination with the cut on his cheek — the one ironically in the same place that he'd marked me.

Unfortunately, the newly-surfaced ego of mine, the one that materializes and grows more after each run-in with Porter, is who surfaces.

Timid and frightened, my mind reels in never-ending loops as it tries to take in every small detail of this scene and figure out what might be about to happen. What sort of mood is he in today? Will he hit me again? Force me to sleep with him? Apologize?

One thing I absolutely can deduce is that by the flattened eyebrows and the downward tilted head, if I run — if I stumble to my room — whatever he has planned will be worse.

"Y-you're back," I stutter, eyes welling with tears as my body and mind begin to shut down.

In some form of miracle, Porter's eyebrows turn from flattened to normal and his head lifts. "Tears? For me?" he states.

I blink rapidly trying to make sense of his unexpected behavioral switch. My head nods in self-preservation while my inner rebel gives him the finger.

The tears *are* because of him after all. Not *for* him, though. But if the line is fine enough that he can't tell the difference, who am I to point out the mistake?

It gives me just enough power to suck in a recovery breath.

"You got out of there pretty fast last night," he states, pushing off the bar top and stalking down the hallway toward me.

"Y-you're surprised?" I respond, despising the tremor in my voice. "The blue-lights were coming. Jude would have killed us both if I was caught on scene." In this little dance we often choreograph, I move a step back for every step forward he takes.

Does he realize I set him up? Or does he think it's his own fault for not knowing the road well enough?

My back hits my closed door. He bumps against me, looking down his nose at my much-shorter form. His hand slips past my left hip and the creak of the door handle echoes through the hallway as he turns it open.

In a movement so fast my head swims, he grips my wrist, yanks me away from the door, then shoves me through, slamming and locking us inside.

I land forward on hands and knees and quickly flip to my butt in an attempt to gain balance and scurry backward. Out of desperation, I choke out, "Jude is in his room right below us."

Porter cackles quietly and taps his back pocket. "Got a text from him that he was going to get some sleep. Unlike you, apparently he stayed up worrying about me last night, and you and I both know he sleeps like a rock."

Blood drains from my face as my upper back slams into the nightstand and the tips of his shoes bump into mine.

Crow's accusations echo in my head.

Not a victim.

Not a victim.

Not a victim.

Then do something, Remi!

With an extended hand, palm out, I whimper, "Stop." The request is pathetic. There's no forceful delivery. No backbone.

Porter raises an eyebrow and laughs. "Remi, Remi, Remi. This isn't a game of Red Light, Green Light." He lunges down, hand outstretched.

Instead of cowering or turning submissive like in the recent past, I finally react: my foot launches up and out and makes direct contact between his legs.

Knees pressed together and hands cupping himself, Porter freezes. Rather than the hopeful glossiness of pain in his rapidly-blinking blue eyes, a fire burns. The kick hit him square on, but it didn't debilitate him or serve as a warning.

Instead, it swelled his anger.

I cannot retreat; he would never let me past. And even if I did manage to shuffle around him, he would catch me. I regret and hate the sudden fight response that came over me.

How dare it.

Fighting makes things worse.

I should have known better.

This could be over already.

Head shaking frantically, hand covering my muffled gasps, I silently plead for mercy as my brows curve inward and tears well in my eyes.

There's no room for forgiveness in his anger-fueled gaze — only rage and retaliation. This time when his hand darts out again, it connects. His fingers wrap into my hair, and he yanks me off the ground.

I'm expecting to be tossed onto the bed, but Porter has different plans this time. He shoves me against the closest wall, twists me around to face him, and grips my chin and jaw. This grip is different than ones before — gentler even despite the roughness in his eyes as they drop to the evolving bruise on my cheek.

"There are plenty of inventive ways to manage you, Remi. I like seeing my marks, but it doesn't have to be that way."

Never in my life would I have imagined wanting him to hit me again... opposed to any alternatives. I know in this moment whatever is about to come will be worse. So much worse.

I jerk my head to the side, but he corrects its angle, fingers biting against the flesh over my jaw.

When I try to dip down and duck away, he presses his body harder against mine with a snigger.

His hand drops to my neck, fingers wrapping around and applying just enough pressure and upward motion that limits my air supply without leaving marks, just as he promised.

Then, with a quick strike, his knee slams into my stomach. I crumple forward. Using the pressure around my neck, he prevents me from landing on the ground. Even as I claw at his fingers, his strength is overwhelming as he tosses me onto the bed.

This part I can handle.

This part I know.

This part...

...I can close my eyes and go somewhere far far away until he's done.

CHAPTER ELEVEN

Jude

Aloud bang startles me awake. I shoot up in bed, eyes darting around the room as my brain tries to wake up the rest of the way and figure out what caused the sound. The soft thump of footsteps — more than one set — can be heard coming from above me. I tilt my head backward, gaze arching to the ceiling.

Remi's room is directly above mine, and though it seems the building design prevents most sounds from traveling through — conversations and the like — steps and other types of heavy movement can be heard through levels.

I swing my legs off the bed, slip on my track pants, and leave the room. The bright light coming in from our floor-to-ceiling windows nearly blinds me as I walk toward the stairs, rubbing my hands over my face and through my hair.

Someone is up there with her. I told her to wake me up if Porter got home because I really want to start keeping a closer eye on what business he takes care of. After Dad died, it was easy to let him help handle everything. I just couldn't deal. Hell, he did way more than help. Porter was a business partner but also my best friend. More times than I can count, he lifted my chin and slapped me on the back, refusing to let me drown in sorrow.

Remi needed me, too. But even giving her the time, attention, and support she deserves has been a challenge. I suppose that all makes me a selfish bastard.

The mental name calling — that chosen insult — stings.

But, hey, if the shoes fits…

Point is, moaning and groaning will not bring Dad back, and partying and sleeping won't run a company. Porter has earned a break for everything he does for our family. Remi needs her brother back.

These thoughts pile up with each step I take up the stairs to a seemingly empty floor. No one is in the fireplace room or kitchen, and down the hallway Remi's bedroom door is closed. When I step out onto the deck to check there, there is no sign of anything amiss.

A muffled sound travels down the hallway. I spin around, straining to listen but immediately try to reverse the action. Before we left California, I promised Remi that if we all lived together, I would respect her privacy. Even though Dad was gone and I felt the need to upgrade from brother to father-figure, I would try not to be too protective and overbearing.

It's hard.

So. Damn. Hard.

Especially since something is definitely going on with her. I had thought that maybe giving her some responsibilities was too much, too soon. But every time she comes back home or texts me after being on the job, she seems happy.

The bruise I noticed on her cheek this morning, though? That is a fucking concern. My promises don't include turning a blind-eye if she gets into an unhealthy relationship.

"But you think every relationship I'm in is unhealthy," she had chided once. *"You're my brother. Pretty sure I'll never have your blessing."*

Which is not entirely incorrect.

Battling with the ethical dilemma, I fall into the recliner strategically placed in the darkest corner of the room. Then, I wait. Just like Dad would.

With that one simple, silent statement, he'd put the fear in us. There was no better way.

Showing up after you'd been out past curfew?

Walking in the front door on report card day with anything less than a B+?

Rumor getting around that you got pulled over but it was only a warning?

Dad would be in this chair, and you wouldn't see him until the moment you thought you were getting away with whatever misdeed had been done.

The leather would creak as he leaned forward, ready to hear your reason. Not ready to discipline, but ready to hear your side of the story before choosing a fair sentence.

Not that I'm thinking about chastising Remi. Nothing like that. She is an adult; I am her brother.

But if the person in her room is the reason for that bruise on her cheek, someone else will be getting punished, and I sure as shit won't be as kind as my dad. Dad acted as judge, jury, and executioner. I'll jump right into the executioner's role.

So... I wait.

I wait a long ass time.

Whatever noises woke me up had stopped a while ago. But whoever was in there, stayed.

Until they didn't, and the creak of Remi's door opening echoes down the hallway and curves around the wall, landing heavy in my lap.

Strung high, ready to pounce, I lean forward carefully so as not to trigger the rub of leather.

Much to my surprise, Porter emerges, walking with a casual stride past the bar and around to the island. I plop backward into the chair again, head falling against the cushioned top, and close my eyes for a recovery heartbeat.

When I open my eyes again, he is leaving the island and rounding the corner to head toward the stairs. His gaze lands on me, and he jerks to a stop.

"Sunuvabitch, Jude. Don't pull that shit on me."

Yeah, Porter was used to Dad's methods, too; he's practically family after all. Dad even pulled it on him a time or two when his mom was expecting him home, but he'd escaped to our house and snuck inside.

"Heard some movement coming from Remi's room. Guess that brotherly instinct kicked in. I was ready to put someone in the grave." I laugh and shake my head. "Fuck… I'm losing my damn mind, man."

He leans against the corner of the hallway, looking down at me, soda can in his hand. "She couldn't reach something in her closet. Tried a few times, made a mess, then threw a Remi-styled tantrum."

We both laugh at that. Get her frustrated enough, and she still does the fist clenching, foot-stomping thing. It's rare, though. "Well, that explains the bang that woke me up and the footsteps that followed."

"Right. Then, she broke down." Porter's mouth curves into a small frown. "So, I stayed in there with her until she calmed again."

I drag a palm down my face and let out a heavy breath. "Hey, thanks for being there for her."

"Anytime, bro. Who were you expecting, though? One of the Revelry crew?" he asks.

My entire body tenses. "Wait… Revelry crew? What the hell are you playing at?"

He huffs out a snort. "Come on, Jude. How do you think she got those plate numbers to begin with?" He takes another drink, lifting an eyebrow over the can.

The original plan wasn't exactly to do a hostile takeover. More like… an election. But give me reason to let out a bit of steam by unleashing some hell on these kids? Sign me up.

I search Porter's face for any hint of deception. Unfortunately, the cuts I find there rush what happened last night back into the forefront of my mind. I shoot to my feet, pushing the idea that my baby sister is fucking the car crew we hired her to investigate to the back of my mind. "Damn, man. You look like shit. How are you feeling, by the way?"

"Better… now," he answers, taking a swig of his drink and darting a quick glance down the hallway.

"'Stang in the shop?" I ask.

"Yeah, took a taxi here. Insurance is still working out the details for a rental." He pushes off the wall and continues toward the stairs.

"Oh hey…" I call out, leaving the judging seat. He looks over his shoulder but continues his path to the stairs. "I'm ready to get back to work. You've done enough — acting as a temp CEO in addition to your already intensive CFO stuff."

Porter nods, takes another swig of his soda, and disappears down the stairs.

CHAPTER TWELVE

Remi

For a very long while, all I can do is stare at the clock on my bedside table. The numbers blur through my tears as they click from minute to minute.

Every time I try to move, my stomach contracts and heaves, threatening to vomit. The impact of Porter's knee hit just right, accosting my body in the worst way; the rough and painful fuck, accosting my spirit in the worst way.

Thoughts speed through my mind.

So many thoughts.

Thought.

Thought.

Thought.

Thought.

When the tears become too thick, rendering me unable to see the time any longer, I resort to curling in a ball, shaking, hands clasped over my head, desperate for the maddening thoughts to take a single lane or exit entirely.

An hour, maybe more, goes by before I'm finally able to stand and drag myself into the bathroom. Every movement, every breath is slow and controlled.

Control — such an abstract term.

An action that denotes power.

A skill.

A tool.

Or, in my case…

A mechanism.

One of coping.

I refuse to allow my body to expel the result of his harsh treatment. Not yet. Not here where he could possibly hear the result of his version of control.

When I get out of the shower, not only do I pull out my best comfy clothes, because I'm not sure I can wear anything else right now, but I pull out several more outfits, too. Tops, bottoms, underwear — I shove as many items into my travel backpack as possible.

With a clenched-teeth, frustrated scream, I punch my fist inside the bag, fighting with the mound that refuses to fit beneath the opening, and finagle the zipper on both sides, up and around my fist, until all I have to do is slide it out to finish closing the pack.

Then, I sling the bag over my shoulder and pitch a leg out of my bedroom window.

Freezing mid-straddle, I realize my clutch is still on the damn bar. Chin up, shoulders back, I change routes, moving to my door instead. My rebellious confidence instantly cowers when I turn the handle, though. She leaves me, and my knees wobble. If it weren't for the door holding me up, I would fall to the ground.

Please let Porter be downstairs. Please.

Eyes closed, like a child who still has the "If I can't see you, you can't see me" mentality, I open the door, step into the hallway, and take a terrified peek.

Porter comes into view immediately. I begin slowly closing the door again when a hand slides across the bar top near my clutch to pick up something on the surface. Jude.

Knowing Jude is there comes as an immediate relief. Porter won't do anything to me when Jude is around, so I walk out in sweat pants and a baggy shirt with my hair up in the messiest of messy buns and a twenty-pound backpack hooked over my shoulders. Instead of rolling my shoulders inward to compensate for the weight of my luggage, I let it act as a support beam, keeping me erect to give the illusion of boldness and confidence.

When I arrive beside Porter, eyes on Jude, the very air circulating is different — oppressive, dangerous.

I grab my clutch, move my backpack around to the front of my body, and open the frontmost pocket. In spite of the pocket bulging, I wrangle my clutch into the small opening while Jude and Porter watch.

"Going somewhere?" Jude asks, his tone just slightly less than brotherly.

"Yeah… I need to get away. No clue where I'm headed, but I promise to text."

Jude's hands grip the counter, knuckles turning white from the force. But he nods nonetheless, calm and collected.

My attention darts to Porter who appears impassive at best. He might have broken me today, but he didn't make me stupid. Not yet. He clearly said something to Jude. Something that pissed him off and was meant to get between us.

That something… worked.

Jude has never looked at me with so much… animosity? Disappointment? Disgust?

Porter's mouth ticks at the side into a barely noticeable smug grin, but he quickly dips his head and covers it with a cough into his fist.

I walk past them toward the door — never more eager to get the hell away from both of them.

"Jude and I were just hashing out some of the details we learned about this crew you've been looking into," he says. "Well… their inoculation, at least. Trying to see what backing they have."

My feet skid to a halt, but I don't turn around. I simply freeze, staring down at the floor, unable to avoid the torment of curiosity. Not for the sake of sleuthing for a takeover, but because I've enjoyed learning more about these guys at every turn.

The silence in the room thickens. My stomach twists from both the hidden bruising Porter left behind and the anxiousness of learning something about the guys' pasts.

As if what Porter is putting me through isn't enough, he has one more twist of the blade to make. One more ruthless knee to the gut: "About three years ago," he states, "this Burke guy lost his entire family in a car crash. Seems the crash was caused by a street racer. Someone on his crew."

The bile that had been threatening to escape for the past hour-plus lurches to the surface, and my hands come up — one to my mouth, one to my stomach. Fingers digging into the cloth of my shirt, palm pressed firmly against my lips, I simply nod in acknowledgment.

"Remi?" Jude calls out, his voice lowered in concern. "Are you oka—"

"He used the life insurance policy funds to start a street racing club — for the cash events," Porter interrupts.

Of course my mind whirls with questions. Why would he support a tradition backed by danger and death when his family suffered the consequences? Is that why even he, himself, will no longer race? Crow is a walking contradiction.

A fire burns steady inside me — the deep blue fed by Porter, but the light yellow at the top, ignited by this revelation. Angry. Curious. Confused.

My eyes widen as a new revelation dawns on me: the year tattooed on his fingers. Three years ago. A daily reminder of when he lost his family.

"Well," I state, clearing all the emotions from my throat with a phlegmy cough. "That insurance money won't last forever, and it'll take some major business-type skills to support the cash events once their funds run out. Seems you guys have this takeover in the bag."

I've seen a peek into what Crow, Hayes, and Trenton can accomplish, but I choose to keep that to myself. With each of their completely different skill sets, they make quite a fierce team. Maybe there is hope for them after all. I step forward and slide the door open.

"Look at me," Jude demands in a tone that sounds too much like our father.

I turn around in the open doorway, lean against the frame for support, and look at him. He opens his mouth to say something, but stops, choosing instead to walk up to me. His eyes fixate on mine, eyebrows knitted together. Then he drops his voice to a level that only I can hear and says, "If something is wrong — if you need me — text me an x. I'll call you, give you an excuse to get out of whatever situation you're in. No questions asked."

Goddammit, Jude.

That was another thing Dad would do for us: if we ever found ourselves in an uncomfortable situation but we didn't want to risk being caught contacting a parent, we had a code. I'd only ever used it once. A single x. Dad texted back stating that something had come up and I needed to come home right away. I flashed my phone to the people I was around and got out of there... with no stain on my reputation or pride.

In my own, small way of keeping him on his toes, I dart a glance over his shoulder in Porter's direction. The smallest of hints. Then, I meet his gaze and give him a sharp nod. If I stand there any longer, no good will come of it, though. I simply turn around and rush across the deck, down the stairs, and to my bike without a single backward glance.

CHAPTER THIRTEEN

Running on a fuel made of self-preservation and determination I pull off on a side road about a quarter mile away and park out of sight behind an apartment complex to check my bike for another tracker. It would be foolish of me to assume Porter is above installing one again.

Once confident there's no way I'm being tracked, I dig out my phone and do a quick search for Burke Halston, aka Crow.

Despite having an unread notification from Hayes, my flight instinct demands I seek refuge through Crow for reasons I'm not yet ready to unpack. Texting him directly is always an option, of course, but my unstable emotions can't handle rejection right now. Let him reject me in person. If he does at least that's one more male I know to cut ties with. Whittling my circle down, one toxic guy at a time.

The search for Crow's address comes up quickly, which, in his case, is a bit terrifying. If I was able to pull the details so easily, Jude and Porter will be able to, also.

Address and route determined, I shove the phone back into my bag and get the hell out of there.

Normally, I love cruising on my bike — the thrum of my tires over asphalt, the wind against my skin. This time it's agony. Every bump, every lean, every time I have to stop and go again, the persistent nausea makes my eyes water behind the visor, and my palms become clammy on the handles.

When I turn onto the intended street, I blink away the sting in my eyes, clear the hint of bile in my throat, and roll my shoulders to work out the ache from carrying both the backpack and my problems.

The address leads to an old workshop with a seemingly abandoned house a distance behind. If it weren't for the familiar, black Supra parked inside the open garage and black-clad feet and legs weren't sticking out from underneath, I would have kept riding.

Instead, I pull into the driveway and park, watching as Crow's knees bend and he switches the pressure to his heels so he can roll out.

As I get off my bike, he sets down the tool he'd been holding, sits up on the creeper seat, and swipes the back of his hand over his forehead before picking up a nearby ball cap. He puts it on backward, hands cupping the sides to adjust its fit, before his eyes finally find mine.

That one look is all it takes for all the accumulated pain, heartache, and anger to bubble to the surface. Knowing that I'm here with someone who knows about the situation with Porter and who doesn't want me to be a victim — someone who cares, maybe not about me, but about me getting out of the mess — causes all the withheld bile in my aching stomach to thrust toward the surface.

I almost can't remove my helmet fast enough and Crow nearly doesn't push off the rolling mechanic seat in time. Somehow, we both manage. My helmet lands with a sickening scrape on the concrete, and I make it to a small strip of overgrown weeds just in the nick of time to expel everything I'd been holding in.

My shoulders become lighter as Crow removes the pack that still hangs heavy on my back. The breeze licks my damp neck as he collects loose strands of hair and reconstructs the messy bun my helmet had pressed down uncomfortably against my crown.

Weeks worth of pain, regret, and guilt leave me and land in a rancid puddle on the ground.

Crow waits patiently at my side until everything is out — until all my insides have spewed the disgusting and volatile remnants of things otherwise best left unsaid.

Apparently at some point he had stepped away and returned, because when I'm done, he has a damp rag ready and waiting for me to clean myself up with. In a wordless thank you, I brush my fingers against his as I take the cloth from his outstretched hand.

While I wipe the cloth across my mouth, he wraps his arm around mine and helps me stand. When I finally take that inhale and exhale of relief, he scoops me into his arms and brings me to his bare chest, ripe with the scent of grease and sweat, and hugs me tight until the remaining tension seeps away... For a time.

When he is ready, not the other way around, Crow lets me go and steps back far enough so we can finally look at each other. His eyes scan my face. For marks? Proof?

My anxiousness returns, suddenly preferring the bruise on my cheek over the hidden assault. Now, all I have is my word. With Crow and our shaky start, words just might not be enough.

"He get more creative?" Crow breaks the silence. A tremendous amount of worry drains from my tightly coiled muscles despite the bite in his tone.

Throat raw, I croak out a pathetic, "Yeah."

"You scared enough yet?" he asks, fists balling at his sides.

I press my lips together, hating the approach. If I confirm his suspicions, it means a strike on my pride and that Porter won. If I deny my fear, it lends to me being an idiot.

Crow huffs and turns around. "Nope. Still fearless, I see. Like a child." There he goes again, calling it. Being more right than he should be. "Fear isn't a weakness, Remi." Crow doesn't look at me, but moves into the garage instead and aggressively begins cleaning up everything he had taken out for his project. "Fear... means you're smart. It's the part of you that tries to save the rest of you from making mistakes."

He tosses my used rag into a can at the corner of the garage, places his tools into some drawers, walks to a sink, and scrubs his hands. "The smartest racers don't push away that fear. They embrace it. Keeps them more alert. More careful. It's the ones who ignore or misinterpret it that get... hurt."

My gaze drops to his hands as he swipes a shop towel off the table and begins drying them off. The numbers stand out starkly against his skin. I want to beg him to keep talking, to tell me more about this interpretation of fear he has with the hopes that he'll share the secrets he keeps so close.

But unwilling to share my own would make me a hypocrite, too.

He steps closer, one slow foot at a time, eyes searching, assessing, judging. Just before he gets to me, he tosses the rag to the side, and it lands haphazardly half-off of the dusty table. He then curves a finger under my chin and tilts my head back.

After a quick glance down to the backpack he'd placed near my bike, his eyes meet mine and he says, "You did the right thing." That gunmetal gaze drops to my mouth and back up again before he steps away and motions over his shoulder for me to follow.

"C-can I park inside?" I squeak as he begins to disappear toward the far back.

"Yep," he responds. "Pull the garage door closed when you're done."

CHAPTER FOURTEEN

Instead of the entryway leading into a mudroom or the first floor of a home, this one opens to a single room. The size resembles a studio apartment but is much smaller. More like how a prison cell might be designed, minus the toilet, of course. There's a futon, small dresser, mini fridge, and a table. On the floor beside me, familiar large black boots are lined up, tips pressed against the wall. I remove my own shoes and nudge them next to his, toes curling against the cool, dust-free concrete.

His apartment is the epitome of what a bachelor shop-worker needs. Nothing more.

Crow is sitting on the edge of an open futon, arms propped on his thighs and head clasped between his hands. Based on the bunched sheet and haphazard pillow placement, I assume he seldom uses the futon in its seat form. When he hears the door latch, his gaze lifts and he gestures toward the corner of the room with a jerky tilt of his head. "There's a bathroom through there if you want to clean up."

With my new, uncertain life packed and hooked on one shoulder, I hustle toward the temporary escape, seeking refuge from the immediate, debilitating sense of not knowing what will happen next.

Recovery comes in the form of a thorough face washing and teeth brushing. Glancing in the mirror, I quickly discover I don't care for my reflection. For that reason, I try not to linger any more than necessary. I look every bit the woman who has the universe attacking her at every turn: my dark brown eyes are muddied instead of sparkling, skin is mottled and puffy, and the mark on my cheek has changed color and is now fading.

In a way I miss the bruise, as twisted as that seems. The colorful bloom told a story. Served as a reminder. Kept me on my toes. Now, the story it penned and illustrated is turning into nothing more than a memory — the truth invisible and subjective.

When I finally work up the courage to leave the bathroom and face Crow again, he is still in the same spot on the futon. He drags a hand down his face, lifts his hat, musses his hair, and puts the hat back on before looking at me. My heavy backpack hangs at my side, nearly cutting my circulation in the two fingers I have hooked through the loop.

Putting the backpack down makes my stay slightly more permanent — makes me come across too weak and needy. Not yet ready to make the commitment, especially if Crow sees me in such a light, I curve my fingers tighter around the loop. I still don't even really know why I came here — why I chose him and not Trenton or Hayes.

Based on his seemingly exasperated expressions and actions, the longer I stand here in a staring contest with him, the more I worry I made the wrong choice — a viral trend in my life as of late.

In case Crow is battling with trying to find an easy out to send me on my way, I handle it for him. I break our eye contact and rush toward the exit. "You… You were closer. Thank you for letting me unload a little." Remembering Trenton saying he had to work, and I sure as hell am not about to bring all my baggage into The Crowbar and Grill, I finish with, "Now that I'm feeling better and can ride easier, I can go to Hayes."

My free hand twists the knob, and the door opens an inch before a tattooed arm reaches past me and slams it shut. The backpack hanging from my fingers slips and falls to my feet as I spin around and press my back against the door.

Crow cages me, a hand pressed on either side of my head. I look up at him, doing my best to keep eye contact and not cower.

"Hayes can't handle you right now," he rumbles.

"What the hell do you mean by that?" I spout, tilting my head back more in defiance.

Both his hand and eyes move to my chin, thumb and gaze dragging across and upward toward my mouth. "When I said you were poison earlier, I meant it. Everything about you."

"If I'm so toxic, why do you touch me the way you do?" I ask, my cheek leaning into his palm as his thumb reaches higher to tug at my bottom lip. I whisper, "You look at me like you despise everything I am, but when your hands are on me, your touch proves differently."

While I'm talking, his eyes watch my mouth move. When I stop, they lift to mine, tongue dampening his lip piercing, preceding his response: "Because even poison in the right amount can save a life. But right now, you're too high of a dose for him. If he sees you like this — still raw, still shaking, still controlled by the man who did this to you — he will OD."

My breath hitches. In a roundabout way, Crow has managed to tell me everything yet nothing at all about Hayes. My voice becomes notably lower and breathy. "I don't know what to do. Where to go. Who to talk to. If I can't go to Hayes and I made the wrong choice by coming here—"

His head dips and breath fans over my ear and down my neck. "See… you've got it all backward. You came to me, not the other way around. I don't need to tell you what to do — you're already doing it. What you need to figure out is the role you want me to play. What do I need to be for you right now, Remi?"

My pulse gallops behind my ribcage. I want to scream, "I don't know!" but not a single sound comes from my mouth.

Crow assists, his voice lowering and pausing with each suggestion. "An ear?… A shoulder?"

Beside my head his newly grease-stained, trimmed nails scrape against the wooden door as he curls his fingers into a fist.

"A protector?" His nose falls to the top of my shoulder and drags a slow line up my neck. "A distraction?"

My body answers for me, head tilting sideways to offer more of myself.

Instead of his nose, I feel the faint coolness of metal as he drags his bottom lip along my earlobe. The hair along that side of my body lifts, every inch tingling.

His hand drops from caging me in, and he brings our foreheads together. The rigid plastic from his backward hat lightly depresses into my skin. Eyes locked with mine, his fingers slip beneath the hem of my shirt and trace lightly along my side as he lifts the material up and over my head, separating our foreheads just long enough to do so.

I hadn't bothered with a bra beneath the baggy t-shirt. It felt far too restricting and too confined at the time, when all I wanted was to be free.

As he brings his hand back down, he skims along the side of my neck, over my shoulder, and down my arm before slipping his fingers between mine and directing my hand to his belt. If I want that distraction, he intends on making sure it's by choice, not by force — on the off chance he'd read my body language wrong.

In a wordless "yes," I lift my other hand to aid in the task. It doesn't take me long to unhook his belt, unbutton his pants, and loosen the zipper.

The stiff plastic from his hat leaves my forehead as he dips his head down and connects our mouths, sinking a finger under the waistband of my sweatpants and tracing a line from hip to hip before sliding his palm around to the small of my back.

His opposite hand scoops beneath my thigh, and he bends his knees in a quick bounce for leverage as he lifts me up. To support the motion, my legs naturally wrap around him. He drops the first hand from my lower back down to under my other thigh, turns us around, and gently lays me down on the futon.

CHAPTER FIFTEEN

C row's steely gaze travels from my face, to my breasts, and lower, until they land on my pants right along with his hands. His fingers scoop under the waistband, making sure to dip deep enough to collect my underwear, too. Then he slides them down, removing them completely before tending to his own clothing.

While he slips out of his jeans and boxers and puts on protection, my own traveling gaze scans his bare chest. I had wondered how much of him was covered in tattoos, and I quickly learn that everything stops just below his shoulder. The finger tattoos stain one hand, and a sleeve tattoo of tire treads marks him from bicep to elbow.

Porter's revelation about Crow's past flashes into my mind. Seeing his ink does nothing to dampen my curiosity. Questions claw at my throat. Not only do I want him inside me, but I want to get inside him, too. I want inside his head. If I'm poison, I want to swim through his veins and learn all there is to know about who he is.

There's no good, logical reason why. There's no sane reason why I'm spread open, exposed to him, both emotionally and physically as he climbs on top of me, situates between my thighs, and presses against me.

His hand lifts and he pushes the wild strands of hair off my cheeks, his gaze searching my face, piercing and probing. With that one little touch, he grasps my heart and soul like he might a shift lever, but when the tug comes to switch gears, my body stalls: when his shaft grazes against me, throbbing and ready to drive us home, my head tosses to the side and entire body locks, knees attempting to slam together but blocked by his hovering body. Images of Porter above and inside me assault my mind.

My breathing turns quick and choppy. My head pounds. The room spins, and everything blurs. I clamp my eyes shut. Hot, firm fingers slip between my cheek and the pillow and turn my face back upright. "Open your eyes, Remi."

I shake my head and press my lips together, but a whimper still squeaks past them.

Crow tries again, shifting his hips back slightly. "Open your eyes. Right now," he insists.

My eyes pop open, wide and begging. Crow locks his gaze on mine and adjusts to lying on my side rather than over me, propping up on his elbow. He moves his hand over my waist and tugs me to roll me to my side, facing him.

"You can't let him control you from a distance like this. Not twenty-four hours ago you were in bed with Trenton and Hayes. Whatever he did to you today…" He clenches his jaw. "He got in your damn head, Remi. That was the only part of you he hadn't ruined yet. Don't let him get away with it."

Tears explode from my eyes, and I curl into a ball and begin to sob. Crow scoops me against him and holds me tight, being the shoulder he'd offered instead of the distraction.

We stay like this for an indiscernible amount of time until I'm all cried out. When I am ready to separate from his hold, he senses the change in my body and pushes up off the futon, the both of us still completely naked. He gathers up his clothes and mine, places mine on the edge of the futon, and heads into the bathroom. I steal the opportunity alone to get dressed.

It doesn't take either of us long to get back to the state we were in before.

He exits the bathroom, fully clothed, and puts his boots on. "Come on. You still need that distraction."

Wide-eyed, I watch him warily as I stand and follow suit, toeing into my shoes. He picks up my backpack and carries it out the door, tossing it into the passenger seat of his car. Then he gets into the driver's seat and turns her over.

As I open the garage door, I learn that at some point during my breakdown, the sun had lowered significantly and now threatens to set.

Since my backpack is taking the passenger role, I assume he means for me to follow him on my bike. I pat at the pockets of my sweatpants to make sure my fob is still in there, slip the helmet over my head and clip the buckle. By the time I'm situated, he's out of the garage and waiting for me on the street.

We drive a while until everything that makes the beach a busy location is well behind us and the area becomes more and more sparse. Businesses, homes, and traffic turn into trees, fields, and power lines. After a final turn, he leads me down another few miles before finally pulling onto the side of the road.

I get off my bike, remove my helmet, and tuck it under my arm while he gets out of his car and approaches. "You been out here yet?" he asks.

"Nope."

"This is one of the hotspots for digs." Crow leans against the rear bumper of his car and shoves his hands into his pockets.

A small smile lifts the corner of my lips. "Is that a challenge?"

He chuckles and shakes his head. "No. Figured you might want to ride WOT for a bit."

The half-cocked smile on my face spreads into a full-blown grin. "Yeah? What's the layout?"

One hand comes out of his pocket and he rubs it over his mouth and down his chin. "Perfect." His gaze drags down my body and back up again slowly. My throat goes dry. His seems to do the same, and he clears the scratchiness away, returning the hand to his pocket. "Hardly ever any traffic, straight for miles, flat, well maintained."

My heart stutters, struggling to keep up with the excitement at the thought of being able to ride WOT. Last time I rode wide-open throttle was before Dad died. As the saying goes, "Hold it WOT until you see God, then brake."

For a while after Dad died, I toyed with the idea of skipping the braking part entirely. For that reason, I have since kept to the speed limit and avoided anything reckless. That is until last night's incident with Hayes and Porter.

"Yeah?" I squeak and bounce on the balls of my feet.

Crow chuckles and shakes his head in amusement. "Yeah. Since you're not familiar with the road, if you want, I'll drive ahead and shine my headlights before the next curve, that way you know when it's coming?"

I peer down the stretch, not at all missing the fact that street lamps are far and few in between. But instead of the oncoming darkness triggering a flight instinct — instead of that fear Crow had mentioned rising to the surface to protect me — a shot of adrenaline plunges through my veins, bringing with it visions of a blacktop visible only by the web of my head light while the road disappears under my tires and the air stings my arms.

"Really? Hell yeah!" My body shakes with anticipation.

"There's one condition." He straightens, stepping toward me and piercing a needle into my bubble of excitement.

Eyes squinting against the final light show of yellows, oranges, and reds across the sky, I raise a single eyebrow.

He removes the helmet from under my arm and fits it over my head, flipping up the visor before stating his terms: "You leave Porter at the line. He has no place in your head, bed, or tread."

The vibration of our connection penetrates every layer of my helmet until I swear I can feel the heat of his palm searing my skin. "I-I'll try," I stutter.

"Huh. You never came across as the trying type. Guess I was wrong."

I lift my chin. My entire helmet and his hand lifts along with it. "Fine. Yes. Porter stays stalled at the line."

Crow's fingers curve firmer inside the lip of my visor and he draws my face down, bringing the top of my helmet to kiss the plastic of his backward ball cap.

His eyes bore into mine through the visor. "Ride hard and don't look behind you — you're not headed that direction."

HE INSTRUCTS ME TO give him a five-minute head start, flashing his phone as a reminder that I can call or text him if something crazy happens between now and then. As he drives off, I hurry to get my own phone out of my backpack just in case.

Holy shit, he was right; there's not an obstruction in sight. The red glow of his taillights is the only thing visible for a long while — much longer than expected. The lights eventually disappear, though, at where I assume must be either the start of the curve or a small hill.

Being alone in the now-dusky light on a desolate road surrounded by trees concerns me far more than riding wide open does, so I bide the rest of the promised minutes by digging my phone out, ready to respond to Hayes's text with a clearer head.

Earlier, I hadn't even bothered to read it. Based on what Crow had said, that was probably a good, subconscious decision on my part.

:Hayes: Drinks at The Crowbar tonight? Trenton said he's got a twenty-dollar tab with your name on it.

A tinkle of amusement comes from my throat and ricochets off the nearby trees, filling the dead quiet with something that sounds a little like happiness.

:Me: Some strange guy took me out to a back road somewhere. Send help.

:Me: Kidding. Kind of. I'm on Steel Field Road with Crow. Should I be worried?

:Me: Oh. And yes to drinks. Hell yes.

My string of messages goes seen but unanswered for a couple minutes, and I worry I won't get a text back from him before I ride out.

I tap against the side of my case waiting not so patiently. The time on my display indicates I've been waiting for six of my allotted five minutes, so I lock my screen with a sigh and start placing it in my bike's storage compartment when it vibrates in my hand.

I quickly swipe the screen back on, grin beaming, and read the reply.

:Hayes: Burke being… nice? Oh shit. Get out of there while you can. ;)

:Hayes: There isn't a meetup at the bar tonight, so I'm going early. See you when you're done being ruined by Crow.

The messages fall to a natural end. I quickly tuck my phone safely away and hop on my bike.

Once ready to go, I roll into the lane. That stretch of time was all it took for the retreating sun to douse the streets in blackness. Crow had said don't look back, but in that, I waver. My eyes flick down to my mirror, and I stare at the red glow of my rear light in the darkening night. With a deep breath, I say a mental goodbye to Porter before returning my focus on the road, speeding up until all the slack is removed and opening the throttle wide without caution.

Without fear.

CHAPTER SIXTEEN

As Crow promised, the road is straight for miles. The back of my shirt comes untucked at some point and the loose material whips maniacally, exposing me to the night. So as not to obscure my vision or embarrass myself more than I already have, I press forward a bit and keep the front of my stomach flush against the base of my gas tank, thus securing my shirt.

But, you know what?…

Fuck it.

Wide open.

Of course, at the speed I'm going, Crow's headlights appear far too soon. Don't get me wrong, the ride was amazing. But my heart crushes a little when it's over.

Crow is parked in the opposite lane at the start of the curve that would have undoubtedly killed me had he not been acting as a marker.

I rev-match with every downshift to make the high-to-low rpm transition as smooth as possible and maintain traction. Then, I dip her side to side just for fun.

Thankfully, my shirt drops along with my speed as I approach, flip a u-ey, and roll to a stop beside him.

Just as I am placing my hands on my helmet clip to unbuckle it, the sound of his engine revving pierces the quiet night. My hands freeze for a heartbeat before dropping back to the handles.

Tilting my head down, I narrow a glare at him through the visor. His top teeth flash before dragging over his lip piercing and curving into a smug grin.

Crow flashes his lights, and my eyes go wide.

This man. He is seriously out of his mind. I can't help but laugh and shake my head. But, hell, if he wants to play, bring it.

My hand slides to my lower back so I can tuck my shirt, but my fingers hesitate over the material. Scratch that. Lips twitching at the corner, I rev back, letting my girl give a warning of her own.

Since he's the one initiating this dig, I wait for the horn, balancing on the balls of both feet so I can lift them quicker. Heart gathering momentum at the tease of racing against Crow and his Supra, I can't help but glance sideways. His tattooed knuckles wrap around the wheel, illuminated by the glow of his dash lights, and his free hand palms the center. When his forearm tightens, I jerk my attention back to the road a fraction of a second before the horn blares.

Once.

Twice.

Three times.

I am not a racer, but I know enough about my bike to run it clean and not fight wheelies and spinning tires. Let the bike do the work.

My rear tire does chirp a bit but I leave smooth nonetheless. However, the fact that Crow's Supra has more traction off the line easily gives him the lead advantage.

Unfortunately for him, my bike's power-to-weight ratio comes in handy after the initial jump. Knowing my mid-range punch will take him, I upshift until we're neck and neck.

We both steal glances at each other.

The opportunity to screw with him is prime.

Instead of leaning forward, I straighten slightly and allow my shirt to fly up and expose my breasts.

For the sake of safety, I don't dare pay close enough attention to wait for his reaction. Instead, I casually pull my shirt back down and tuck it tight, then I lean forward and return to the task of murking him on the street.

He'll fall back on straights like these against a decent bike every time.

He knows it.

I know it.

His lights reflect in my mirror, but I don't dare take my eyes off the road. If he meets me nose to nose again, then it is what it is, but until then I'm not going to bother.

Now, should we draw this past the next curve, he might catch me on the lean, but if the race ends before then, he doesn't stand a chance.

A bit of dicing takes place for a spell, but then he suddenly goes from nearly perfectly adjacent with me to at least a car length ahead. With my throttle wide, there's nothing more I can do to take the win. His rear fishtails, and he's gone.

I start the downshift process, straighten, and suck in a breath—

Hold the damn phone.

After exhaling the first recovery breath, I take another deep pull of exhaust-filled air.

Sulfur.

That...

Fucker.

He hits the brakes and slowly pulls onto the side of the road, but his peacocking isn't over yet: the Supra's engine revs high and is followed by a flashy spit of fire from his exhaust.

Race over, I move to the legal lane, close the distance, and pull up behind him, jumping off my bike as quickly as possible, ready to retaliate.

My helmet is off and balanced on my seat before another three-horn blare could start a rematch. Stomping toward his car like a fitful child, I point an accusatory finger at him as he gets out, fox-like grin spread across his face.

"You used your fucking nitrous!" By the time that last word falls from my lips, my finger is poking his chest. It rises and falls under my touch, and only then do I notice the wildness in his eyes.

"You played dirty first," he breathes out raggedly as though the race was on foot not tires.

"Y—" I've got nothing to counter with, so I pin him with a glare instead.

His eyes dart rapidly between mine, chest still heaving. Remembering his panic attack the other night after what went down with Porter, his admittance to not racing anymore, and what Porter had said to me about his past, I grab his face between my palms and bring his nose close to mine.

He closes his eyes, hands launching up to grasp my wrists. When his grip tightens and I think he's going to tear my hands away, in one quick motion, he slings them behind his neck and slams his mouth against mine, arms wrapping around me, hands splaying over my back.

He steps forward and I step back, the two of us engaging in a messy dance as we try to get to the front of his car. Once centered between the headlights, he breaks the kiss long enough to lift me up and place me on the hood.

Our eyes meet as I rest on my elbows and he leans over me, bringing his mouth a breath away from mine. I arch up, swipe my tongue along his piercing, and probe between his lips until he softens against me like he did at the train tracks.

It doesn't take long, but it doesn't last long either. The kiss goes from zero to sixty in less than a second.

It's not pretty.

We struggle.

Out of our clothes.

Out of our heads.

Every act is desperate and rushed because each of us knows that in the state of mind in which we find ourselves, there's no time for second guessing. We want it enough to take it before the logical side of our brains kicks in and this leads to a dead end.

He helps me balance on the edge of the hood, tearing off my shirt while I fight with the belt and zipper of his jeans. My hand wraps around him to tug down the back of his pants, but something thick in his back pocket gives me pause. Realizing we're going to need protection, despite our hurry, I dig out the wallet and pull back, leaning on my elbows again for support as he yanks off my shoes and tugs at my sweatpants and underwear.

His eyes lift from a downward tilted head and he acknowledges with a sharp nod that it's okay for me to dig around in there.

In the dark, I can hardly see anything inside, but I know the familiar square package tucked away in one of the pockets is what we need.

I pluck it out and swiftly return the wallet to his back pocket, lifting my hips concurrently, to aid in him tugging the cloth past my ass.

As he pinches the foot of my sweatpants and slips them off entirely, I tear open the package and toss the wrapper, holding the condom up in the moonlight to flip it to the correct side. Me completely naked and him jutting out, his knees and shins meet the bumper, hands wrap around my waist, and he pulls me toward him. I crunch up, slip the condom onto his tip, and roll it down.

Neither of us waste any time after that. Our eyes lock, both making a silent statement that if we want to pull out, now is that time. When neither of us move to escape, he leans down for a breathtaking kiss as he thrusts inside me with one thorough, drawn out pump. Burying himself. Reveling in the vise of my pussy around him for the first time.

As fast as we'd worked to get here, time seems to still for several heartbeats. The buzz of rapid activity floats away, and the sounds of our caught breaths and the chirrup of bugs in the trees sharpen.

Then... they disappear again. Crow straightens and my ankles lock around his waist. His fingers dig into my hips, and he slides out a few inches, then slams back inside me like that shot of nitrous he'd bested me with.

Just like that, time speeds up and we buck against each other like the finish line is too far away and our lives depend on getting there as fast as possible.

It isn't pretty.

It isn't sweet.

It's a purge.

We're driven to the end faster than our dig lasted. In a heartbeat, we're sweating, sticky, panting messes on top of his hood.

Reality comes crashing down on us, and my eyes spring wide, meeting his. I flash my teeth in a grimace. He drags a hand across his jaw, tattooed knuckles covering his mouth.

When he drops his hand and reaches out to help me up, his expression is shuttered. I accept his offer and he assists me off the car, further aiding in collecting my belongings before tending to himself.

I gather my clothes, step away from the beams of his headlights toward the woods, and take on the task of getting dressed.

Crow does the opposite, taking off his shirt and moving to his door, bending inside, and pulling something out.

A bottle of water, I realize as a faint trickle meets my ears over the sounds of nature.

He returns to his hood, damp t-shirt in hand, and buffs the sex off his car.

A grin quirks up on my lips.

Fucking car guys.

CHAPTER SEVENTEEN

T he door chimes, and I'm taken back to the first and only other time I've ever been inside The Crowbar and Grill: the night I met crew Revelry. Well, not Crow yet officially, but he was there. The second time was for a short meetup, and we only hung out outside after the bar was closed.

Since we're here much earlier tonight than the two times prior, the restaurant side is still open; families and couples are sprinkled throughout the dining area eating dinner, wait staff is hustling about, the jukebox is playing oldies, and Trenton is slinging drinks behind the bar.

Crow and I do not blend in. He's shirtless, and I'm wearing sweatpants, a pajama shirt, and donning wild hair — for several reasons at this point.

Looking over the heads of his current bar patrons, Trenton spots us coming, and his mouth pops open at the state of our attire. Crow stalks toward the end of the bar that has regular stools instead of fake motorcycles — opposite from where I had sat before.

Hayes turns to see what Trenton is gawking at, and he chokes on the drink he'd just taken a gulp of.

"No shirt, no shoes, no service. You know the rules, man." Trenton hides his grin behind a fist.

"Fuck you," Crow responds. "Go get me your after-work shirt."

"Right away, Grumpy Bear." Trenton disappears into the employee area and comes back with a ball of neon-pink cloth which he precedes to toss directly at Crow's face.

Crow catches it, eyeing the offensive color with a groan. Beggars can't be choosers and all that, so he pulls it over his head and pushes his arms through the sleeves.

The color is just so not him. I manage to hold back a peal of laughter… until I read the graphic: "Any day can be Taco Tuesday."

Understanding Trenton better the more I hang out with them, I'm well aware his reasoning for owning this particular shirt likely has nothing to do with the food type of tacos; rather, the other kind you can "eat." Flirty and filthy all the way. I love it.

Crow gives me a super serious side-eye, and although I try to press my lips together, it doesn't work. My mirth still breaks free.

Hayes leans forward to look at me around Crow's glowing personality — ahem, shirt. "Steel Field, huh? Did you race for shirts or something?"

Crow rolls his eyes, leans forward, ass lifting from the stool, and steals a bottle of liquor from the other side of the counter. "If that were the case, she'd be the topless one. Not me."

Trenton yanks the bottle out of Crow's hand, replaces it with a glass of ice, and waits patiently for Crow to straighten the glass so he can serve him.

He fills the glass slowly, tracking it out of the corner of his eye while his attention turns to me. "What can I get you?"

"Sex on the Beach, please."

"Ah, shit... sorry but my shift doesn't end for another few hours. How about a drink to pass the time?" Trenton adds a cheeky grin to the foray.

Crow lifts the tumbler and chugs the contents in one go, ending the debauchery of his libation with a growl and slamming the glass onto the bar top.

"Tell us how you really feel, Burke," Hayes pokes.

Trenton slides a napkin onto the bar in front of me and places a colorful, tall beverage on top.

My attention returns to Crow, his behavior brewing a mix of embarrassment and anger inside my veins. I want to place my hands on my hips and say, "That bad, huh?" but I let out a huff and wrap my hand around the icy glass, instead, ready to drink away what happened on the hood of his car, clearly just as much as he is.

Either the sound or movement, I'm not sure — perhaps both — draws his attention sideways again, and his eyes drop to the string ring on my finger. It's worn but somehow still hanging on. By a thread. Kinda like me. A lot like him.

Moreso, the ring serves as a reminder that he just screwed the girl his best friends are interested in.

His gaze lifts to mine, and I remove the orange garnish from my Sex on the Beach and place it between my teeth, slurping out the juices loud enough for all three guys in my party to hear.

Crow breaks eye contact, and I return my attention to the pretty concoction, only to find that Trenton had replaced it with a bowl of orange slices.

Hayes laughs. "Keep it up, Crow. T-Top is having way too much fun at your expense."

Crow grunts and greedily pushes his empty glass toward Trenton. Trenton alternates an inquisitive glance between the two of us before acquiescing to Crow's caveman-like demand.

I pick up one more orange just for kicks and put on a quick show for Trenton as he tops off Crow's drink. He puts the bottle behind the counter and tries to nonchalantly adjust his hard-on, lest customers see anything.

"Wait…" Hayes breaks the awkward, uncomfortable, mix of humor and tension. "You… raced?"

Hayes directs the question at Crow. Trenton was seconds from breaking away to check on some customers down on the other side of the bar, but he freezes mid-step and spins around.

Both men wait for Crow to answer. His head tilts down, and he suddenly becomes very interested in the golden liquid clinging to the ice in his tumbler. Then his gaze lifts and meets Trenton's across the counter, and his pointer finger taps against the glass, lips pressed in a fine line.

Trenton's eyes widen impossibly large. "Did she best you? Is that why you're so pissy?" Trenton chortles.

"I would have if he hadn't raced dirty."

"She would have if she didn't cheat."

"You juiced?" Hayes asks him aghast.

"She was asking for it," Crow grumbles.

Hayes leans back so far on his stool, I fear he'll fall off, once again looking around Crow at me. "What did you do?"

"Nothing."

"She flashed me."

"My shirt came untucked."

"It was on purpose."

"Your eyes should have been on the road."

"You're a distraction."

"You weren't complaining afterward…" This last volley comes out as a whisper.

The entire restaurant seems to fall silent. Everything freezes in time like it had when our bodies joined. Logically, I know it doesn't — that the world is turning beyond our back and forth — but nothing can be heard except for the buzz of tension between us and the drum of blood pulsating in my ears.

The entire time, Crow keeps his eyes on Trenton. Something to focus on other than me. Trenton stands there, fingers curled on the edge of the bar top, in a silent battle of wills with one of his best friends.

I haven't yet seen that sort of look on his face — the type of emotion he's capable of outside of his humor and loyalty.

And I also can't translate it. Not like Crow and Hayes can. Trenton darts a glance at Hayes, and Hayes pushes out of the stool, reaching behind Crow to drag a finger along my lower back.

Tearing my attention away from Trenton and Crow, I meet Hayes's glasses-rimmed eyes, and he jerks his head toward the exit.

I step down but only make it three paces when the sound of something clattering onto a metal surface draws my attention back toward the bar. I twist a glance over my shoulder and spot Crow's car keys sitting in the seat I had just vacated.

Throat tightening for no damn good reason, I double back, yank up his keys, and storm out of the restaurant, Hayes on my heels.

CHAPTER EIGHTEEN

Hayes follows me wordlessly out to the parking lot and around back where Crow and I had parked beside the Bimmer and Monte Carlo.

Since actions speak louder than words, I decide to take that approach, unlocking Crow's car, snatching out my backpack, closing the door, and turning to Hayes.

When I'm just a few feet in front of him, illuminated under a parking lot lamp, I drop the backpack at my side, straighten my shoulders, and lift my chin. Despite the attempt to appear defiant and bold, my throat trembles around a difficult swallow.

Hayes's eyes dart back and forth rapidly between mine, trying to pull everything from me all at once without a single word spoken.

It's the unavoidable redness in my eyes, and the quiet sniff, that moves him into action. He bounds forward, wraps his arms around me, and squeezes tight.

It only lasts a second before he holds me at arm's length and scans every inch of me. "Are you okay?" he asks with a slight mix between a squeak and growl in his tone.

"Better than I was this afternoon," I admit.

His hands drop and fingers curl into fists. "You went to Crow?"

Biting at the inside of my bottom lip, I give him a hesitant nod. My fingers twirl Crow's key chain relentlessly until the rapid friction from the metal burns my skin.

Is he upset because he's worried something is wrong with me? Or do his hands tremble and clench because I ran to Crow?

"Good," he says with a sigh.

I toy with the idea of spewing out all my excuses, but that's not typically how I work, and I don't want to start now. Plus, if I act guilty that means I probably am.

Problem is, the questions are all there in his eyes. He wants the excuses. Every one of them.

I cave easily to his silent request.

"He was closer."

Hayes nods.

"He kept my hair back while I threw up."

His jaw moves over clenched teeth.

"He offered to distract me."

He swallows hard.

"He held me while I cried."

His hands loosen, color returning to his knuckles.

"He took me out for a ride."

That's where his expressive responses end. "Did you challenge him?"

"No, he flashed his lights and revved."

"And nothing bad happened? It started and ended. He won. You both played dirty."

"Right."

"So then why is he so fucked up in there, Remi?" Hayes raises his voice and points a finger behind him at the building. I can tell the abrasive reaction is because he cares about his friend and isn't directed at me, but my heart cracks nonetheless, and I flinch at the accusation.

He rubs a hand roughly through his hair. "Sorry," he amends, dropping his voice back to normal. "I assume since Crow gave you his keys to get your backpack, he hasn't exactly agreed to let you stay at his place tonight?" he asks, bending down to pick up my bag. The weight alone implies the severity of the situation, and he stumbles to counter the unexpected heaviness.

"I… never asked. You and Trenton offered. If that offer still stands, I can maybe crash at your place. Take things one night at a time."

"Yeah. Let me put this in my car. Then we'll talk… right?"

"Right."

I stand alone in the middle of the back parking lot as he walks to his car, pops the trunk, places my bag inside, and we walk together to the restaurant's small outdoor deck at the side of the building.

On the way, I begin to explain everything that has happened from the moment I left their house to when we arrived here at The Crowbar.

Having been warned by Crow that Hayes might not handle the news about Porter well, I gloss over those specific details, but not in a way that lessens the severity of what Porter had done. Rather, I'm just careful not to make it too graphic or bring my fear and emotions into the mix for Hayes to feed off.

When I mention the part about almost having sex with Crow, he doesn't even flinch — not an inkling of disappointment crosses his contemplative expression.

I'd been hella worried despite putting on a confident outer facade. In the throes of passion with Crow, I wasn't exactly wondering how extensive their willingness to share went. After the fact was a different story; I hated the idea that I possibly ruined what was only just beginning with Trenton, Hayes, and me.

There is no set commitment. Nothing official. We are all still in this strange, amazing, honeymoon phase. Yet still… single… in a way?

Anyhow, Hayes's understanding and focused attention makes getting to the part on Steel Field Road a lot easier to stomach. "We… We weren't thinking straight. High on adrenaline, low on our internal battles. We used each other. Hit it and quit it."

Hayes laughs at that, and I feel lighter instantly. I love this open-style communication they all seem to have. And I love that they included me in the mix.

"Clearly you don't know Crow very well."

"You're right. I don't know him at all."

"Well…" Hayes adjusts in his seat and bumps his knee against mine. "He held you." A grin lifts his cheeks. "Crow doesn't 'hold' people."

My own laugh trickles out at the image of Crow embracing random people.

"He joined in last night. He's never included himself in our extracurricular bedroom activities," Hayes further explains.

I raise an eyebrow at the choice of terms.

His voice lowers and shoulders droop. "Crow hasn't raced in years. There's a reason, but it's not mine to tell."

He reaches out and places a hand on my knee. "Once Crow 'hits it,' there's no quitting. We'll work through it. I'm just glad we all happen to be friends who want the same girl. If it were anyone else, you'd be causing wars."

I roll my eyes at him. But little does he know, that statement isn't too far off base. I am, in fact, in the middle of a war.

"Ready to go see what Trenton was able to pull from Crow?" he asks with a wicked grin.

"Oh? Was this a good cop, bad cop thing?"

"Something like that."

"Who the hell was the bad cop?"

149

"Trenton, of course."

I blow a raspberry from my lips. "Trenton? Bad? I'd have to see it to believe it."

"Yeah? Well let's hope you never do," he says tucking me into his side and placing a kiss on my head.

CHAPTER NINETEEN

Whatever information Trenton pulled from Crow, both men are tight-lipped about it. Not even several drinks later does Crow loosen up any. He gets so plastered, though, that both Hayes and Trenton refuse to let him drive. And, much to his bemusement, instead of depositing him at his own place, Trenton makes Crow come with us — with the promise that as soon as they finish "wearing Remi out," he and Hayes will leave to get the Supra so it's at the house by the time he wakes up in the morning.

When we get to their place, Hayes offers up his bed to Crow, nonchalantly insisting he doesn't mind sharing Trenton's bed with me... and Trenton. Crow declines with an adamant shake of his head. "I'm not getting in a bed with her," he slurs. "Might not ever get out," comes next under his breath.

If I were desperate enough, he wouldn't be safe on the couch either. But, I keep that little tidbit to myself.

He throws himself onto said couch, tossing a forearm over his eyes as though the dim lighting is positively offensive.

Is it terrible of me that I very much want to screw with him while he's so amenable? Filled with amusement at his expense, I dart eager glances at both Trenton and Hayes, nearly bouncing on the balls of my feet.

Trenton leans against the hallway corner and lifts his customary, after-work bottle of beer in a blessing of sorts. Hayes sits on the chair beside the couch with a grin.

Crow is still mumbling curses about me under his breath as though I'm not standing right here within earshot. I slowly and quietly get on my knees beside his head. "Burke," I whisper. His arm flies away from his face, and he goes cock-eyed, his gunmetal-gray eyes nearly crossing from my close proximity.

The smell of whiskey washes over me when he opens and closes his mouth in shock. "Don't call me that," he states, eyes zeroing in on my lips.

I adjust to sit on the floor beside him, knees bent and angled to the side. The backward ball cap he's wearing is presently popped off his head slightly since he's lying on the bill, so I take it off all the way and toss it onto the nearby coffee table.

"The name suits you," I say, running my fingers through his hair to fluff the parts the hat had plastered to his head.

Everything about Crow freezes except for his chest which rises and falls beneath his borrowed, neon-pink shirt, and his gaze which travels over my face and along my arm.

"Why the nickname 'Crow'?" I ask.

His eyes flick up to mine.

"No? I don't even get that much?"

He shakes his head.

"Were you engaged in a murder?"

Trenton snort-laughs over near the hallway.

"Weapon of choice, a crow bar?" I add.

Crow's eyes narrow.

I pull my phone out of my pocket, place it on the floor near my feet, and dial his number discreetly. When his phone vibrates, he unfreezes, lifts his ass up a little, and digs it out of his pocket.

When he sees my name on the screen, his gaze narrows again, and he rolls his eyes.

I grin. "You're not going to answer that? I was just *cawing* to say thank you." Even despite the humor, the thank you part is wholeheartedly honest. For the distraction, the shoulder, the protection.

This time Hayes chuckles. Crow's focus cranks over his shoulder, and he pins him with a glare. "You guys are seriously going to let her bully me like this?"

It's my turn to laugh. The sound returns his attention to my face. "How's it feel to be on the receiving end for once?" I raise an eyebrow in challenge. He has been trying to help me, but his methods are very bully-like, and he knows that. Now I get to have a little fun.

His lips press into a thin line, and he places his phone down on top of the tightening of his pants. "I have enough poison in my blood right now; don't administer anymore." The confession is surprisingly sober and coherent.

"Guess we should both sleep it off, hm?" I ask.

He nods in agreement, side-eying me warily.

"With that hard-on, try Counting Crows. That might help relax you a little." Since I just can't stop, I poke fun again, this time turning the popular sheep counting game into the old band name.

The tick of an amused grin twitches the corner of his lips.

Yes! I busted through his grumpiness.

The tick disappears just as quickly as it appeared, though. He props up onto an elbow, reaches his hand toward me slowly, his upper body and face coming awfully close to mine.

The scent of whiskey washes over me again as our cheeks graze. I'm expecting a whispered, sexy remark. Something unbridled and loose because of the alcohol. But he doesn't say — or do — anything where I'm concerned at all. He scoops his hat off the table behind me and falls back onto the couch, places the hat over his face, and crosses his arms over his chest.

Hayes stands and holds his hand out to me. I take it, scoop my phone off the ground, and allow him to propel me upward.

Since I have quite a bit of my wardrobe and toiletries shoved into my backpack, I pick it up and make my way toward the bathroom to get ready for bed.

The first thing I do when I get into the privacy of the bathroom, though, is unlock my phone and open up the messages to text Jude.

:Me: Staying at a friend's house again. Probably for a few days. I need some time away.

Nerves bounce around in my belly as I wait for Jude's response. To pass the time, I start my bedtime routine.

Soon, the phone vibrates, and I snatch it off the counter, eagerly swiping through to my message with Jude. But the incoming text isn't from him:

:Crow: You're welcome.

CHAPTER TWENTY

J ude never responded. Not last night at least. Whatever Porter had said to him may have been exacerbated by the fact that I decided to stay away for a while.

Part of me hopes that while I'm gone, he'll get to the bottom of what's going on under his nose on his own. Surely he can find the truth on paper, somewhere. Or discover the deceitfulness of both his sister and best friend with his own eyes — learn that no one can be trusted, not even blood.

Maybe that makes me a coward.

No… that *definitely* makes me a coward.

And like all good cowards do, I push the thoughts far far away.

When Trenton, Hayes, and I finally emerge from Trenton's room, the couch where Crow had been sleeping is empty. I deflate a little. It's not hard to admit that I had hoped he would still be here. Heck, I even entertained the idea of him sneaking into Trenton's room last night. Or… me sneaking out.

Not that I wanted to sneak away from those guys. Nor that they would allow it to happen.

Even though Trenton sleeps hard, Hayes doesn't.

One thing they definitely have in common, though, is their stamina. Eventually, if we're in this for the long haul, a discussion will need to be had. I am not entirely sure my body can keep up this honeymoon stage forever.

At one point, I had woken up to use the restroom, and when I got back, Hayes pulled me down for a super-early-morning romp.

Trenton slept through the whole thing which, to be honest, was a turn-on in and of itself. Everything with them is a turn-on. But having Hayes clasp his hand around my mouth to muffle my wails while slamming into me… Whew.

I'm well aware he and Trenton prefer to play together. And I love it, of course. But it also reminded me that Hayes has yet to have me by himself. Something I intend on remedying eventually. Sooner, rather than later, hopefully.

I pad into the kitchen and hop onto the counter to watch Hayes do his thing with the coffee science kit. Baggy sweats, big shirt — I'll never understand why he hides all those yummy muscles.

Add those glasses and that messy hair into the mix, though, and it doesn't matter what he's wearing. He has this smart-guy charm about him. The fact that he is a beast in the bedroom makes his whole persona package even hotter.

My eye-fucking is brought to an abrupt end when Trenton pops into my personal space — one that I am most definitely not opposed to sharing with him.

He wiggles his way between my knees, scoops his fingers along either side of my neck, thumbs resting on each of my cheeks, and brings my mouth to his.

Every kiss, every touch of his, is always so sweet, so sincere. So honest and real. His kisses hurt in a good, but terrifying way. He pours all of himself into every swoop of his tongue. Every time.

My butt scoots forward and center presses against him firmer. Trenton groans against my mouth before pulling away and dragging his thumb across my lips. His head shakes slowly and eyes dart all over my face, unsure where to land. What to study. "Never leave," he whispers. "My heart won't handle it well."

His heart isn't the only thing that won't handle it well, if the erection pressing between my legs is any indicator. "You mean your bed, I presume?" I whisper back, gaze and lips brushing against his mouth.

"That too." The response comes as a tickle of breath against my lips.

My fingers had been curved around the counter's edge, but I let go to push them over his shoulders and clasp around his neck. Then, I draw him into a hug, wrapping my arms around him entirely. His hands drop from my face and scoop around my lower back, tightening around me like a vice.

I rest my cheek on his shoulder and close my eyes. Lost in the moment, everything around us drops away. Everything except the truth: that I am still a threat to them and keeping secrets is equivalent to telling lies.

These guys don't lie. They wear their hearts on their sleeves. They're loyal. Almost to a fault. I don't deserve them. Not by a long shot.

When my eyes finally open, my vision is blurry, and a single tear escapes. Hayes comes into view, coffee lifted to his mouth as he watches me crumble silently.

I blink repeatedly and pull back from Trenton, dropping my gaze and hands to my lap, hoping he doesn't catch the faux pas.

He doesn't. But only because the front door flies open, and all our attention swings that way. Crow traipses in, food in hand once again.

Trenton's eyebrows shoot sky high. "Two mornings in a row? We're blessed with your bubbly presence and food on back-to-back mornings?"

Crow huffs and empties the bags onto the table just as he had done yesterday, refusing to make any eye contact. "Eat or don't. Doesn't matter to me one way or another," he states.

Trenton races around the bar, and I hop off the counter. Hayes hands me my coffee, and we approach together. Everyone takes the same seats we had yesterday. Crow's knee bumps mine, and a silly blush tracks across my cheeks. A visible one as the return smirk proves.

I push my mug to the middle of the table between us, but this time he pushes it back. "After you."

So, he had been watching and realized I hadn't even gotten a chance to drink any yet. That, or he is making sure I haven't literally poisoned him.

My attention flicks to Trenton and Hayes; they are watching Crow, amused. Trenton gives Crow a squinty side-eye, but Crow isn't paying any attention, the unwrapping of his sandwich taking priority above all else.

I lift the mug and take the first, hot sip, pushing the liquid to the back of my mouth so it doesn't burn my tongue. Then I place it between us again. This time he does accept it. But then he throws me for another loop by twisting the mug around, and dragging his tongue along the part of the rim my mouth had just been before taking his own swallow and returning it to the table.

Fire ignites between my thighs, and I draw my knees together. Or at least try, but his black-booted foot is between mine, knee pressing against me, preventing the closing of my legs.

When my eyes flash upward, he's immersed in his sandwich, nonchalant as though absolutely nothing is going on under the table.

This…

Drives me wild. In the best way.

He is a horrible human being.

The worst.

The type I can't stay away from.

A perfectly formed, not at all tainted sensation of what his cock felt like inside me last night on the hood of his car fills me, and my inability to counteract the throb with the press of my thighs is torture.

He has warned me not to let Porter get into my head, but what about him? He's in there. No matter how much cold, hard distrust he displays toward me, all I can entertain is the image of a man who held me, the two of us completely naked, while I trembled in his arms and washed his chest with salty tears. The ultimate trust. Two people, clearly driven by a need to be with each other, but as soon as I broke, he had more patient control than I would've ever expected.

I finish chewing my bite with difficulty and take a drink of the coffee to wash it down. The heat leaves my cheeks and detours to my chest and lower. My pussy throbs and aches unfairly.

At the hint of desire, Trenton and Hayes will take me right away. There's no pussyfooting around. No waiting. None of this taunting. The ache right now is so strong it has more control over me than I have over myself.

I now fully understand why some men just can't keep it in their pants. If they feel this way, it's a damn miracle they can put on pants at all.

Body seeking contact, my butt scoots toward the edge of the chair, shoulders moving downward closer to the first bar of the ladder back. I scoot down until his knee is no longer grazing the inside of my leg but has full contact with the part of me that controls the rest.

I do have a mind enough to be fleetingly grateful he is tall and I don't have to bury myself under the table to get the friction I'm so desperate for.

He'd done well to keep his focus on his meal, but I am not remiss to notice the evil smirk that lifts his lips around the next bite when he realizes my desperation.

That smirk only grows when he pushes out of his chair to stand, refusing my body's wishes. I nearly slink down in the chair completely but manage to right myself before the other two men who own my body notice.

A redness covers me from cheek to chest for an entirely different reason now.

Yep. He is the worst type.

I hate him.

I glower in his direction as he steals my — our — coffee, chugs the rest, and places it in the sink.

Hayes pushes his still half-full mug my direction, and I turn even redder, should that be physically possible.

Horny, angry, and now embarrassed, I've lost every bit of my appetite both for drink and food… and sex. My eyes track Crow as he moves to the couch, plops into the middle, stretches his arms over each side, and throws his head back.

Trenton breaks the uncomfortable silence by standing and collecting all the trash. "I open today, but you kids have fun here. Don't do anything I wouldn't do," he states.

Crow had angled his head to look over his shoulder toward the table when Trenton began speaking. When Trenton added the part about not doing anything he wouldn't do, Crow's gaze flits to me for the briefest moment before he returns to his reclined position, eyes closed. "There's not much you won't do, T-Top. You sure you want to leave her unattended?" Crow asks. "Hayes, don't you have to be somewhere today too?"

Hayes turns his head toward me. "Yeah, I have some business to take care of. Will you be good here for a while?"

"Yep," I squeak out. "Crow, You're leaving too, right?"

Please say yes.

"Nope. You're stuck here with me."

The room falls silent. Even Trenton freezes, seconds away from disappearing into his room to get ready for work.

"Hang out here often?" I ask, picking up on a major vibe that he doesn't usually just hang out here. Or bring food over.

He has nothing to say in response. Instead, he shrugs everything off, eyes still closed.

166

"I… I have some errands to run, too," I announce. I don't, but I'll find something to do.

Staying here alone with him is not a great idea.

Not at all.

CHAPTER TWENTY-ONE

Leaving their house does nothing to get my mind off Crow's curious behavior. That man is a damn roller coaster ride.

Doesn't help that roller coasters are my favorite amusement park feature. Or that I quite enjoyed riding him. With him. Both. In his car and on his cock.

In a way, I feel like I owe him something, though. That part I don't much care for; I don't like owing anyone. It's something I learned early on lurking in the shadows of the industry — bad things happen when debts are due.

In a rough, roundabout way, Crow helped me. A lot. That's not saying my troubles are over… Far from it. Porter is not gone. The problem is not solved. But Crow is great at giving me reminders of my worth or to what standard I should hold myself, even if he's an asshole with his approach sometimes.

Whether I want to cut ties with him or tighten them, I am not entirely sure at this point.

Yet, as I wander around town, really getting to know the area for the first time, an idea starts to form. An offer of truce that could make whatever is happening between us worse or better. Time will tell.

Hitting up a custom print shop, I waltz in and pitch my idea to the girl behind the counter. She assures me it's an easy job and should be ready in just a couple hours.

Ironically enough, the shop is near the marina — the very same one where Trenton drove his fingers inside me while Crow and Hayes drove circles around us. I decide to waste time there for a while, working through my demons.

The whirlwind of events since we arrived in this new town had been enough to distract me on occasion, but it had also served to open my eyes a little. Shown me that sometimes not everything is as it seems.

When I park near the edge where the concrete drops into the depths, the scene doesn't trigger a flashback. Perhaps it's because I'm here during the daytime rather than night. Whatever the reason, I'm able to envision what had happened the night my father died, allowing myself to replay it step by step for the very first time.

Doing so is probably a terrible idea: about midway through, I want nothing more than to jump off the ledge and sink to the bottom of the bay, never to be seen or found again.

The twenty-four hours preceding my father's death, unease had skittered up my spine. Simply recalling the memories of that night causes that same skitter to return.

As I leave the marina, my eyes catch once again on the cameras Trenton pointed out, and that skitter turns to an icy dread.

I don't let it linger, though. After all, I have a custom order to pick up.

And so I do just that before returning to Hayes and Trenton's house. Hayes is back, but Trenton is still at work. Crow is nowhere to be seen.

I don't much care for how his departure disappoints me. Hours ago, I couldn't stand the idea of being here alone with him. Now I'm wishing he had never left. Ugh, that man makes me crazy.

After I finally get my stuff all situated and tuck the custom gift I ordered for Crow behind some kitchen appliances, I find Hayes holed up in his room. When he opens the door, he's shirtless and glistening in sweat. Evidence of his exertion is outlined on the bench of his weight set. He steps back and gestures me inside.

"You sure?" I ask. "If you're busy, I can just hang out in the living room."

"No, ah… I was just finishing." He swipes a hand through his damp hair.

Our relationship, or whatever this is, is still so new that even though it's no-holds-barred in bed with him, there's still this lingering awkwardness sometimes. It tends to bounce off him and attach to me, resulting in this giddy school girl and boy dynamic.

My foot nearly turns in in that cutesy awkward twisty move, but I straighten to correct the posture and take the short few steps inside his room instead.

He closes the door behind us even though no one is in the house. Out of habit, I suppose.

I sit on the bed while he moves around the room, opening drawers and tucking different items of clothes under his arm. "Um… I'm going to take a quick shower. I have games on my computer. A stereo in the corner. You're welcome to whatever you can figure out how to use."

I raise an eyebrow. "Are you questioning my ability to understand all your fancy electronics?"

He laughs. "Hmm… Maybe a little."

"I do like a good challenge, you know."

This gives him pause. I mean, he runs the financials of an underground street club after all. Hayes thinks about the possible repercussions of his free-range offer for a moment before stating, "Well, if you can access the stuff that I have under digital lock and key, then I suppose you deserve the information."

He's definitely calling my bluff. I am decent on a computer but likely not nearly as proficient as Hayes.

Just for fun, I continue to let him think that maybe I could crack the code on all his secrets by feigning general disinterest yet flashing a devious smirk.

But when I stand to approach his computer, I turn and approach him instead. Because the real priority right now is touching his chest while he's all hot and sweaty.

Being a head taller than me, his chin tucks to look down at my face when I inch as close as possible. Eyebrow lifted inquisitively, he questions, "Again so soon?"

"Ahaha, a comedian," I respond, looking down at an imaginary watch. "It has been at least twelve hours since your cock was in me last. I hardly think that's too soon to have it again."

Hayes groans and tosses his head back, shifting slightly from foot to foot. When his focus meets my eyes again, he says around a choked breath, "I need a shower."

I inch up on my tiptoes and brush my lips against his. "So do I." But then I step back, turn toward the bed, and shrug, "I mean… if you need to recoup, I get it—"

His arm is around me in an instant, tugging me snug against his warm, sticky body. "A chance to get you to myself? There's no way I would pass that up. I'm more worried about you. Not me. Together, Trenton and I are rarely gentle."

Well… he's right. That's fair. And hot. And the bulging erection throbbing against me is proof enough that he's no longer worried nor needs to recoup.

"Does that mean, you'll be gentle this time?" I ask, pressing our bodies together harder.

His mouth comes to my ear. "Do I need to be?"

I shake my head and tilt it to the side so he can drag his teeth along the length of my neck.

When he gets to my shoulder, he steps away, walks to the edge of the bed, and sits, waving me over. I straddle him, and his hands slide up my outer thighs then scoop around to my ass. I lean my forehead down against his and run my hands down his neck, shoulders, and back, fingers dipping into all the lines and grooves that are slightly more defined since he just finished working out.

"I need to ask you a few questions," he says, adjusting his hips under me, causing his thickness to rub between my legs.

"And I need to give you a few answers," I respond, squirming against him.

"Are you into things like choking, anal, spanking, double penetration, being tied up…" he continues to list several more things in a rush of nerves, but I cut him off.

"I am willing to try anything once. If I like it, you'll know. Like what you did the other night, I

174

definitely liked that. Pretty sure my body proved as much."

"It did." His shoulders loosen. "That doesn't mean we don't read women wrong sometimes. That also doesn't mean our bodies don't occasionally respond against our minds' wishes either. Biology and all. People can come in their sleep; doesn't mean they want to."

Science. Right. "Fair enough. How about this? If I am worried or decide I don't like something, I'll tell you. I have learned being with you and Trenton, that I like the surprises. The non-contractual, unspoken agreements. The way you two make joint decisions but are still careful to pay close attention to how I am wordlessly in agreement or disagreement."

"You've yet to be in disagreement." He throws me a wink and squeezes my ass.

"And I probably won't ever be."

CHAPTER TWENTY-TWO

The short, but to the point, conversation seems to be enough for Hayes. Since meeting, we had all been so consumed — so eager — that none of us discussed anything about what we like or dislike. Not favorite colors or foods and certainly not whether or not I would be cool with things like taking both of their cocks at the same time.

Yeah, we still have a lot of growing to do and a lot to learn about each other.

But considering my self-preservation as of late, I am perfectly happy with the unknowing for now — the bliss shrouded in mystery. It doesn't make me not curious, though. I want to know more about Crow's tattoos. More about why Porter's treatment of me triggers Hayes. More about this apparent craziness and danger Trenton has buried under his facade. More about how they all became friends and what continues to keep them loyally bound in such a passionate way.

More… everything.

We're simply doing things a bit backward: sex first, wine and dine later.

"You may have just agreed to way more than you expected." Hayes's eyes twinkle with mischief as he adjusts under me again, his cock growing harder from both the conversation and friction.

"Story of my life right now," I mumble under my breath, considering the irony.

Hayes nudges me off him and palms himself down, tracking me over the rim of his glasses as I stand.

His gaze drops for a second, eyes closing completely as he takes a deep breath. He looks about as consumed as I constantly feel around these guys.

After a recovery swallow, he opens his eyes again and points a finger at the length of my body. "Strip," he commands. My eyebrow and the corner of my mouth lift in smug amusement, but I cross my arms over my waist, pull my shirt off, and wiggle out of my shorts.

When my fingers reach for the clasp of my bra, he clears his throat and shakes his head. I try rerouting, fingertips dipping into the band of my underwear, but he again interrupts the motion.

Curling his fingers inward, Hayes gestures me toward him.

Obeying, I step between his knees. His hands brush up the outsides of my thighs and over my hips. He leans forward, and his lips feather across my stomach, sending a swath of goosebumps along my skin. While he kisses a line above the waistband of my underwear, his fingers explore the curve where my hips and thighs meet.

My body is not at all ashamed of what it wants. When his exploration dips between my thighs, I'm forced to use his shoulders for support; if his knees weren't bracketing me, my legs would wobble and give way. Or they would spread open, ready for any and everything he wants to do.

Much to the dismay of my unfurling insides, Hayes keeps my legs wedged closed. Lifting his hand and dragging a thumb along the thin material over my clit, he ignites a fire inside me — thumb acting as the match head and using my clit as the striker, a flame of need licks up my core. The material separating us is no longer sexy, but bothersome. I want to feel all of him on — and in — all of me. Attempting to satiate the searing throb between my legs, I remove my hands from his shoulders and bring them to my waistband again.

Hayes is quick, though, grabbing each of my wrists to thwart my efforts. His head tilts back slightly and dark-blue eyes, hazed in the purple glow of his room, look up at me. "Back to my shoulders or I'll have to figure out a way to keep them there for you."

That confidence and take-control behavior in the bedroom still surprises me. Hayes is so often sweet and bumbling. When his cock comes into play, though, a switch flips.

My entire body reacts; a tremor vibrates through me from head to toe at the challenge. Maybe I want him to "figure out a way" to keep my hands from roaming. Or do I want to see what he does to me if I'm obedient?

Both images seem to result in the same physical response, however. My underwear dampens. My legs weaken. My pulse and breathing increases.

As though he can read me well enough to know I'm battling with the decision, Hayes waits patiently for me to make a choice. Closing my eyes and taking a deep breath, I return my hands to his shoulders and dig my fingers into his flesh.

He responds immediately with the drag of his teeth against the sensitive lower part of my belly. It jerks in response, and I squirm between his legs. letting out a pathetic, frustrated whimper.

A breathy chuckle feathers against my skin. "I want you nice and wet before you take me. We can use lube, but what's the fun of that, hm? If your own lube isn't enough to get the job done, I'm doing something wrong."

My mouth refuses to work over the thickening of my tongue, rendering me speechless. He hasn't even made it beneath my underwear yet, and the natural lube he speaks of accumulates.

He stands, scooching me backward. Once his legs are completely straightened, our bodies flush, he dips a finger under my chin and lifts my mouth to his. His tongue traces the shape of my lips, teasing me by not entering even when I lean into it. My eagerness must test his resolve because he inches his lips away from him and takes a shaky breath. Ready to move on, he drops his hand into mine, turns, and pulls me away from the bed.

Without a word, Hayes guides me over the weight bench so my legs straddle each side and I am close enough to grab the metal bar with both hands, leaving me somewhat bent over, ass perfectly viewable from behind.

In this position, with my hands supporting me, it would be unwise to let go. If I do, the only option would be to either fall forward or straighten completely. Neither of which, I imagine, is conducive to whatever he has planned.

As soon as I'm settled to his liking, he drags his palms down the center of my back until both hands cup my ass. I peek at him over my shoulder as he straddles the bench behind me. One hand moves to between my legs, cupping me over my underwear before dragging the tips of his fingers along the material over my clit.

It's amazing how turned on and wet he has made me with only a few touches. Damn. I am so ready. But Hayes is working on his own timeline — gassing me up, while I burn through it faster than he can fill me.

Once again, as though he knows my body better than I do, he makes the next move. Perhaps it was the shake of my limbs or the tensing of my thighs with the last touch. Whichever clue my body gave him, he slides my underwear to the side and drags a couple fingers through my folds.

The ensuing groan proves he is not at all disappointed with my apparent progress. He scoots forward more and leans over me, his mesh shorts and the erection restricted within pressing against my ass. His sweaty chest becomes flush with my back, and he drives his fingers inside me, mouth coming to mine to sup on the quiet wail the action creates.

He straightens again. His fingers continue working my insides curving and twisting just right, revving my body up as high as it'll go without overheating. An orgasm threatens and teases, but he pulls away, stilting the release.

When he is no longer making contact, I look over my shoulder and watch as he pulls his shorts down partway to let his cock free. He removes a condom from the drawer in his nearby desk, puts it on, then scoots forward again, slides my panties aside, and drags himself through my wetness.

My palms build a thin layer of sweat against the metal bar as he slips inside me nice and slow, hands moving to either side of my hips to support himself as he moves forward once more and fills me completely.

His fingers toy with the line of my underwear, dipping under them, lifting, and snapping them against my skin as I press backward onto him, unable to get enough or be filled sufficiently despite his size and expertise.

One hand presses into the center of my lower back, and the other comes up to my bra, finger and thumb finding my nipple and pinching it through the fabric.

Goosebumps trail from my breast, around my ribs, and down my back to meet his opposite hand as he presses the palm of his hand downward in contrast to the upward thrust of his cock.

The fingers twisting my nipple loosen and trail down my side until he scoops his hand over my hip and between my thighs and wiggles his fingertips beneath the fabric to give my clit similar attention.

My entire body seizes at the contact, pussy clenching around him. He slides out, pushes my panties down to my knees, and realigns with my other entrance, fingers quickly returning to expertly work me in slow, rhythmic circles.

Hayes succeeded in conjuring enough body-made lube as promised. Every touch, every insinuation. The anticipation. His full and thorough strokes.

My body throbs with desperation.

His tip presses firm against me, halted by a resistance that's nonexistent with traditional sex, and an extra sensitive, rarely felt bundle of nerves that immediately causes a zing of sensations to course through me. At nothing more than the simple pressure of his girth.

Hayes enters extra slow. Tortuously slow. Ensuring I climb the peak of release with his touch while he takes everything my supple body willingly gives.

The new feeling hurts but in an oddly satisfying way when combined with every other consuming sensation: his slow and languid fingers, the rhythmic sound of his breathing, the back of my thighs sticking to the front of his from the perspiration caused by our efforts.

He pauses and pulls out a little. This new friction is an agonizingly pleasurable contradiction to the stinging pressure of his entrance. My breath hitches and chest heaves, insides so easily on the brink of release. Hayes uses the pliability of my body's eager response to his advantage, entering deeper with the return grind.

This achingly slow and filling process is pleasure defined. Euphoric. Intense. Extreme.

The pain is just the right amount to pressurize me from the inside out. Everything around us goes fuzzy. Thoughts. Motives. Sight. External sounds.

Holding myself up becomes increasingly difficult. The moment he slips in the last inch and our bodies merge, the hand that had been pressed at mid back slides upward, over my shoulder and arm, and he clasps his fingers between mine on the weight bar, his chest now flush with my back again. His other hand is still wrapped around me, fingers shifting against my clit, while his cock drives inside, increasing in speed only when my body is loose and ready.

There is no longer any concern as to whether or not I can take him in this way. Now that he is fully entered, everything that comes next is smoother and easier… and oh so damn good. The friction of his slow and rhythmic grinding mixed with the tension is maddening.

My fingers curl tighter against the bar, and I buck against him, pulling out the first sound he's made during this aphasic experience. Hayes lets out a mixed grunt and groan, the fingers clasped between mine clenching around the bar, the veins on his upper hand and forearm popping from the effort of holding himself up while curved over me. Violent yet protective. Sweet yet savage.

Hell, I can't get enough. Again, I buck against him, and a deep-chested growl trickles out with his next exhale. A shot of pleasure-pain ricochets through my body, and I explode. My hands white-knuckle the bar, and my body heaves and shakes. All my control is lost, completely steered by Hayes. He thrusts hard one more time, cock twitching in unison with the clenching of my release.

When we are done, he slowly pulls out, quickly scoops his arm around me, slings his leg over the bench to gain better footing and lifts me into his arms before I collapse onto the bench, utterly spent and useless.

CHAPTER TWENTY-THREE

Hayes nudges the bathroom door open with his foot and closes us inside with a bump of his hip. "Can you stand?" he asks quietly. I give my wobbly legs a test when he eases me to the ground. Discovering they do, indeed, still function properly, I give him a dreamy smile and nod.

He sits on the edge of the tub and turns the water on, alternating hot and cold until it's a temperature he's pleased with. I lean against the wall, unable — or unwilling — to stand on my own.

After the first task is accomplished, he fills the bottom of the tub with a shallow layer of water, lets it sit for a couple minutes, then drains it. I watch as he takes these methodical steps much like he does with the pour-over coffee technique. It's all very intriguing, but I'm far too wiped out to ask any questions.

He assists in removing my underwear and bra, takes my hand, leads me into the tub, and encourages me to sit in the center. When my bare ass

187

meets the porcelain, I understand why he went through such a process with the water. The bottom is a perfect temperature — not too hot, not too cold; it doesn't shock my senses like I had expected. The water is still running, bubbling near the drain at my feet.

Hayes sits behind me, bent knees bracketing each side of my body much like they did that day on the beach when I had sat between his legs on the sand. He reaches forward past me with an empty cup in his hand and fills it from the spout. After straightening, he gathers my hair in his opposite hand and tilts my head back.

Warm water cascades in a slow trickle over my forehead and through my hair as his lips drag along my jaw before landing on mine with a soft peck.

In the sweetest, most unexpected act, he bathes me first, then himself. Something I hadn't realized how much I needed until he did it. Not the cleaning part — I mean, yeah, I need that too — but the gesture. The care. Tired and a bit sore, his ministrations are more than welcome.

When Hayes and I are clean again, he rinses out the tub, fills it halfway with fresh water, reclines back, and adjusts me between his legs so I can rest against him.

As if the moment could get even more magical, we both fall asleep this way, our skin pruning in the water, warm in each other's arms. The stuff of movies and romance novels.

The saccharin moment twists at my double-dealing heart. Before long, I need to go back home. Make a choice I don't want to make. Ruin everything. Either with these amazing guys… or with my brother.

* * *

I HAVE NO IDEA what time we got out of the bathroom and made our way back to the bedroom, but we did at some point. When I finally stir beneath the sheets, I wake up alone for the first time since these sleepovers started.

What comes as even more of a shock is that neither Hayes nor Trenton woke me up during the night nor the early morning to play. In a way, I'm glad. But that relief doesn't mean I'm no longer interested. I am. A lot. But the break is much needed.

With bleary eyes, I sling my legs over the bedside — still very much feeling the weight of exertion in my limbs and elsewhere — and make my way out of the bedroom to the kitchen. All three guys are hanging out, engaged in conversation. A conversation that stops quite abruptly when I appear from the hallway.

Scanning the situation, my gaze lands on each guy, searching for any hints surrounding them that will tell me what's going on.

There's a fresh bundle of food wrappers on the top of the open garbage can. My stomach silently rumbles, and I press my fist there to help prevent it from getting vocal. The guys had all kept me fed while being a guest in their home, but I never want them to think doing so is expected or required. A self-care plan begins to nudge in my mind, and an agenda for the day starts forming. An agenda that doesn't depend on or require their assistance should they need a break.

First on the schedule — I steal a glance at the time on the stove — a trip to the grocery store or a fast food joint. "If anyone is hungry, I'm happy to cover lunch," I say while taking a mental drive through the streets to envision what food places I had passed yesterday.

The marina and downtown area zoom past in my mental cruise, and I am reminded of the custom gift I had gotten for Crow. My attention flicks toward the spot where it's hidden.

"Crow left you some food on the table," Trenton reveals.

My helpful idea and offer screeches to a halt. "Again?" I ask, unsure how to feel about this uncanny generosity of his.

Trenton explains further, "Don't let his invisible villain mask fool you. He actually threatened to take us out back if we touched the last sandwich."

Crow narrows a glare at him and Trenton smirks.

Hayes huffs and his eyes twinkle in amusement.

When my focus locks on Crow's again, his eyes quickly roll toward the ceiling. "I'm just looking out for their weight. Add too much weight to their cars, and it'll sway the races."

A laugh bursts out of me, and I throw my hand up over my mouth in surprise. I am very well aware that an extra sandwich isn't going to add too much weight to Hayes or Trenton.

Giddy and warm fuzzies fill me from head to toe. A pink blush blooms over my cheeks. "Thank you for saving me some food—" Crow tries to interrupt with a pointed finger, but I continue before he can "—I actually got you something, too." The room falls silent. "Nothing crazy." My attention darts from guy to guy, all of them share surprised and uneasy glances. "No big deal, really." I wave a hand dismissively and approach Hayes, leaning in close to whisper a small request in his ear.

Hayes nods and gets to work, pulling out all the items in his pour over kit right away.

"Care to join me at the table?" I request of Crow and Trenton. Crow presses his lips together, piercing burying between his lips, but he heads to the table nonetheless. Trenton flashes me a killer grin and follows behind.

Wanting to make sure Crow isn't stealing a look, I peek over the bar top toward the table before removing the gift bag from its hiding space. Sure enough, his head jerks back down to cover up his spying efforts. That man is too much like a damn toddler — emotions all over the place, impatient, too cute for his own good. It's hard not to laugh.

Hayes side-eyes me, equally as curious as he finishes grinding the beans and tapping the grounds into the filter. When he pops open the cabinet above his head to pull out a mug, I remove the one I purchased for Crow out of the bag, rinse and dry it, then slide it toward Hayes.

He turns the mug around, tilts it back to study the custom design, and presses his lips together to lock away his laughter.

There isn't much to the design; really, it's no biggie. But... I thought it was perfect and appropriate for my and Crow's morning dicing the past couple days.

I nudge up to Hayes as the kettle starts to whistle and he turns the burner off. Resting my chin on his shoulder, I ask quietly, "Do you think he will like it or be offended?"

Hayes pours the first swirl of water over the grounds and whispers back, "He'll act offended at first, but he'll love it."

Better prepared to deal with Crow's complexities, I nod against Hayes's cheek, step away, and join Trenton and Crow at the table.

Their eyes track me, both of them overly inquisitive as though today is suddenly every holiday rolled into one. As I get comfortable in the seat, I unwrap my sandwich, noting the oblong shape; the garbage in the can was all burger wrappers from what I could tell, as had been the usual lately, but this one is different. A deli-style wrap… and an apple.

I would have never ever complained about his generous meals each day, but burgers have never been my go-to. Wraps, sandwiches, and fruit, definitely, but not greasy burgers.

When I lift the apple to take a bite, Crow reclines, tattooed fingers covering his mouth, steely eyes piercing mine. My eyebrows draw in, and I remove the apple just inches from touching my lips. "Did you poison it? Give me a date rape drug?" I ask, alternating a narrowed glare from him to the apple and back again.

Crow's eyes crinkle in the corners, and his hand drops. "You're already filled with enough poison… and I don't need to give you a date rape drug to fuck you."

My mouth pops open in a small O before I press my lips together and drop the apple onto the table. My eyes dart to Trenton who is resting on an elbow, fist pressed into his cheek. The only thing missing is a bowl of popcorn.

"Dude, what did we tell you about working on that habit of getting up on the wrong side of the bed?" he asks, slapping Crow upside the head with his free hand.

Crow rubs the point of impact. My lips twitch with the effort to not quirk high.

Hayes rounds the corner, gift mug in hand. Crow assesses him, morphing from feral dog to curious cat in an instant. Hayes conveniently has the decal side of the mug facing toward himself, and he strategically places it in front of me in a likewise manner. To Crow, it's nothing more than a plain, white mug.

I opt not to take the first gulp. If Crow insists like last time, I'll insist right back. Instead, I hook my fingers through the handle, spin it around so the design is facing him, and slide it to the middle of the table. A peace offering? A show of... friendship? Something.

Pick your lane, Crow.

At first, he doesn't drop his attention to the mug, choosing to keep wary eyes locked on me instead. I pick up my apple again and lift it in a cheers.

I'll bite, if you do.

His gaze drops slowly to the mug, teeth immediately working into a grind as soon as he sees the design. Six simple black letters on stark-white porcelain: "Cawfee."

Crow swallows hard. My heart skips a beat. Under the table, his knee leaves mine. Just as my heart makes its descent to the floor, the tip of his boot meets the tips of my bare toes, and he slides it around to the side of my foot, lining them up just so. His long lashes splay upward as he glances at me from beneath them.

Then he reaches across the table and accepts the mug. Holding it up in a return cheers.

He takes a gulp, and I take a bite.

CHAPTER TWENTY-FOUR

Hayes

My background check on Remi got put on hold. The day I had started — the same day she ran to Crow for help — I couldn't stop thinking about why she wasn't texting back as quickly as usual. Something was going on, and not being able to do anything about it shot my nerves. All I could accomplish was hitting the weights. By the time her and Crow met up with us at The Crowbar, I was already feeling the ache in my muscles. I had overdone it.

During her visit, it got worse before it got better. To the point where my biceps and triceps fucking burned to even so much as lift a hand to touch her face.

The only time my muscles didn't bother me was when she was distracting my body in other ways. And damn did she ever. Trenton and me both. I never would have thought that a woman could keep up with us. But she somehow does.

Every hour of her temporary stay, our feelings for her got stronger. At least, I know mine did. And if the way Trenton and Crow are behaving indicate anything, theirs most definitely did, too.

Unfortunately, during the downtimes she became more and more anxious — checking her messages constantly, occasionally thumbing in texts that clearly are meant for someone outside of our group. With Crow breathing conspiracies down my neck, the desire to scoop her phone up and spy on her correspondence killed me; I hate that apparently my trust is superficial enough to warrant a want for prying.

But what made me feel even guiltier was when I finally did work up the courage to flat out ask about the messages. "My brother," she said without pause. "I promised to keep in contact with him. And I have. But, I can tell by his texts that he's uneasy because I haven't stayed away from home for this long since before our dad died."

That was enough to alleviate most of my concerns about whom she so fervently replied to. But it also increased my desire to dig up the dirt on him.

Because there is dirt.

I know it with every fiber of my being.

Having her around, though, halted my ability to do exactly that. In the meantime, both Trenton and I tried casually pulling information from her, but the conversations never led to any details that shed light on the gaps we can't fill.

In the least, she is always open to talk; that's one thing we all like about her so much. With our pasts, communication had become our lifeline. Crow, Trenton, and I don't keep stuff from each other — a pact we made a couple years ago and stuck to.

At any given time, one of us might take a right of silence while we work through shit in our own heads — Crow at the present time, for example — but we still make sure to come clean sooner rather than later.

For that reason, we always give each other the benefit of the doubt. For that same reason, we continue to treat her likewise.

I didn't want her to leave, yet in the same breath I did.

For now.

Her leaving means she's going back to the dangerous situation at home. When she walked out the door, the urge to pull her back inside was strong.

However, on the flip side, I now have an opportunity to dig — to get information that might help us help her.

Fast enough to where nothing will happen between now and tonight when she'll hopefully show up at the meet. We all avoided talking about tonight the whole time she was here, so the fact she went back home the same day as our ticketed event, did nothing to lessen Crow's concern.

We all want to trust her, and for the most part, we do. Well... Trenton and I.

Crow is still hung up. The gift she gave him definitely cracked his shell a little, but it also messed him up a bit. "She is fucking shady as hell, Hayes." His voice flows through my computer speakers.

Fortunately, her stay and our conversations did result in gathering enough information for me to at least narrow the search.

A name.

A hobby.

A location.

Little bits here and there.

Enough to start with.

If there is something shady to find, it'll likely be encrypted. I open up my dark web browser. "What, exactly, are you expecting her to do that's so suspect?" I ask Crow, fingers flying over the keys.

He's quiet for too long, and I can't help but laugh. "You've got nothing. So, what if she shows up? What if she doesn't? Which is the wrong move? Because from my point of view, neither really is. She shows, or she doesn't. Simple as that."

"I don't have a fucking clue." He groans.

"Clearly."

We both know what the real problem is, but he continues to plead the fifth. Crow isn't worried about her betraying the club. He's worried she'll break his heart — the one he refuses to acknowledge exists.

Scratch that — our hearts.

"See you tonight," he says, clipped.

"Yeah… See ya…" I respond, words trailing as my eyes scan the queue.

With just a basic search on her father's name — a helpful detail she let slip during a casual discussion about car sales — the reason Remi knows so much about cars is immediately evident: Lance Industries Incorporated.

Lance Industries is a large West Coast company covering several different branches of the automotive industry: manufacturing, sales, maintenance, etc.

Troy Delancey owned repair shops, dealerships, facilities, and warehouses. If it was connected to vehicles, he had a finger dipped in the pie.

Owned — past tense — since he died a few months ago. The company fell into the hands of CEO Jude Delancey, CFO Porter Davis, and CAO Remi Delancey.

Nausea bubbles in my stomach like a freshly tapped into well.

She is a corporate chief executive for a prestigious automotive corporation.

Remi had never once mentioned this depth of her entanglement in the auto industry. She had only said that her dad "….ate, slept, and breathed vehicles," and he had died recently. Well, that information was definitely the truth. No lies there.

If I take my feelings for her out of the equation, it's not hard to admit that company positions can default to a deceased owner's heirs in some scenarios.

My fingers itch to investigate this more, though. To find out just how deep her involvement dives. But I made myself promise to not broach her direct privacy. Not entirely at least. The goal is to find out if there is any incriminating evidence against Jude and Porter that can give us just, legal cause to get her the fuck out of there.

Not that Porter simply existing isn't enough cause. But, I know well enough how that sort of thing works. Interfere at the wrong place and the wrong time, and helping is the last thing that would happen; a sad and unfortunate truth is that 'helping' with situations like this can cause more harm than good if not careful.

Digging a little deeper into Jude and Porter's involvement with Lance Industries, I uncover yet another clue: not only were they involved in the aforementioned aspects of the company, but they were also tapped into the import branch of the industry.

…Which explains why Remi had revealed a tease of her watercraft knowledge that night on the pier.

Fuck.

Damn, Remi.

This is not looking good.

I should stop. Right here.

My fingers zoom across the keyboard as if of their own will. A few minutes later, I have a list of shipment ledgers filling the screen.

The person to sign-off on the last logged delivery: R. S. Delancey. In pretty, curvy writing.

…On the night of Troy Delancey's death.

I was wrong.

There is dirt… But it's on our girl, not her brother.

CHAPTER TWENTY-FIVE

Remi

Moving in with Hayes and Trenton is tempting — so damn tempting. In a silly roundabout way, Trenton had made the offer, waiting on bated breath for my answer. As it stood, I was already unfairly encroaching on their space. Yes, for a good reason — I get it. But besides that valid point, I also need to see Jude again. It had been long enough. He was close to hitting the streets with a search party, despite my best efforts to assure him that everything was fine.

Whatever Porter had said to him before I left, strung every word in every text together with a straining, taut line. One thing he didn't beat around the bush about, however, was his eventual flat-out request for me to come home. Today.

Only when I knew for certain Jude would be home — and awake — and I wouldn't be there alone with Porter, did I finally leave and head that way.

I left my backpack behind since Trenton and Hayes didn't seem to mind. In fact, they pretty much insisted on it. And, honestly, I feel better knowing it's there. A readily stable "Plan B."

The best part about staying with them was that in doing so, I had removed myself from any intermeddling with the clubs. Being at home would mean I'd be expected to continue working. Being at Hayes and Trenton's meant avoiding shoptalk if I wanted, or engaging in it, if that was my preference. I had control. Options. And I opted to stick with simply enjoying their company.

As I open the sliding door to my official residence, I can't help but wonder what's in store. My unorthodox pep talks with Crow and lots of distractions while I was gone boosted my confidence. I feel refreshed. Stronger.

Like I can take on the world.

Like I can take on Porter.

Jude… if I have to.

Both men are here. Both eating dinner. I had avoided coming too early, figuring the more I am forced to linger here throughout the day without something to do, the more opportunity Porter has to harass me.

My plan is to walk in, talk to Jude, go to my bedroom, lock the door, and stay there. All night. All the next day if I have to.

"Hey!" I greet as though I've just had a fabulous time away from home. Because I have.

"Welcome home, stranger," Jude responds, shoveling in a mouthful of food. "Thought you'd moved out for good."

I pull out the stool next to him, sit, swipe a crouton off his plate, and pop it in my mouth.

"What, they don't feed houseguests wherever it was you stayed?" Jude asks, nudging my arm away with his elbow.

"They fed me well. Food off your plate has always tasted better for some reason, though."

"You look… happy," he points out, pushing his meal over to me. I pick up the fork, create the perfect bite, and place it into my mouth. My gaze moves upward as I lean over the plate. Porter's eyebrows are flattened, and he's leaning against the back of the stool, arms crossed over his chest.

I chew the bite thoroughly before grabbing Jude's water and stealing some of that, too. "I had a good time. Was kinda nice getting away from… life… you know?" I flash Jude a grin and pat him on the shoulder. "You should try it sometime. Stop worrying about your hopeless sister. Stop working so hard. Relax a little."

Jude's head bobs. "Maybe I will. After tonight, I might be able to get away with a short vacation."

Porter huffs, but Jude doesn't pay him any mind.

"Tonight, hm? Hot date?" I prod.

"Thought you'd never ask," Jude answers. The smile on his face couldn't be any larger. "Open House is tonight." He lifts his hand and checks the time on his wristwatch. "T-minus two hours and counting."

Blood rushes to my toes, my forehead becomes damp, and my stomach churns. "Your meet is tonight?"

Porter decides now is the time to chime in: "Got big plans?" he asks.

I shake my head in a daze, mind traveling back to that golden ticket. "No," I whisper-gasp.

The "no" isn't in response to Porter's question. It's a verbal denial to a mental war. I'd looked at the ticket. I had seen the date. But I chose to ignore it.

"Great!" Jude pipes up with an added poke to my stomach. I jerk and clasp the still-tender spot. "Go get dressed; we're leaving soon."

"I…" My fingers grip the material of my shirt tighter. "I'm not going."

Porter's jaw clenches, but his lips still quirk up to the side. I tear my gaze away from him before Jude can catch the exchange.

Jude's brows pull together, and he tilts his head to the side, dark-brown eyes boring into mine. "Okay… I thought you said you didn't have any plans tonight…"

"Right. I… I guess after being gone for the past few days, I was looking forward to a chill night here, you know?"

Jude nods slowly, calculating. Porter sits back and enjoys the show; the one where I dig myself out of the grave he buried me alive in.

With a deep breath, I cross my arms. "There a problem with that?" I ask.

"No… I just assumed you'd be excited to see the result of all your hard work."

"The res—" Ohhh it burns. The injustice of it all.

"You single-handedly led us directly to the crew we're going to bring down." Porter grins. "Pretty damn impressive, Remi. On the first night of the job nonetheless. You were born for this."

"Porter is right. All the cred goes to you. Come with us. Celebrate."

My head shakes emphatically. "You both know this kind of stuff is not my scene. Thank you for trusting me enough to bring me into the fold. But… I'm tapping out of this part."

I had lied to Crow: I never penciled in their meet. I also never sought out any more details about this one. The goal? Avoidance. Let me just be a woman the guys met and fell for — a sister of someone who just so happens to deal in automotives. I can't do this tug-of-war anymore.

To keep my hands and thoughts busy, I hop off the stool and collect their plates. If I disappear into my room — if I walk away during the sticky moment — one of them will come looking to finish it. At least by hanging around for a little bit longer, it gives the impression I'm not running… despite the urge to do just that.

CHAPTER TWENTY-SIX

Jude

Remi starts cleaning our plates… by hand. Last I checked, the dishwasher worked fine. Not to mention, she hates that chore. Remi would rather clean the bathroom any day over doing the dishes.

Ten minutes ago she walked in here without a care. The time away had done her a world of good. What changed in the last ten minutes?

Sure, she'd been taken aback by the invite to tonight's meet. Porter and I have been attending meets for years, and we had never included her.

But right now she's… stalling? I replay the entire conversation in my mind, eyes traveling from Remi to Porter in the order things were said, using them as a visual to remember the details.

When I get to Porter, his eyes are locked on Remi, jaw clenched. Sure, I get that he's pissed off about her not going tonight. I feel that. But, damn, if looks could kill.

My attention moves back to Remi. The longer she stands there, the more aggressively she cleans the plates — her knuckles whiter than the suds.

"Well…" I break the silence. She startles, nearly dropping the dish. "We need to get there before everyone else, so I'm going to head downstairs and get ready."

Remi's efforts speed up. She rinses the scrubbed plate and places it on the counter — with the other dirty ones — then turns to me with a forced smile, wipes her hands on her jeans, and nods. "Text me live updates?" she suggests.

"Sure…" I respond, standing.

She tilts her head down and clears her throat, darting the quickest flick of a side eye at Porter before walking away from the sink…

…the long way…

…around my side of the table, behind him, past the bar top, toward the hallway.

Porter remains seated, eyes locked on the spot where she had just been standing.

Remi makes it about halfway down the hallway, when something comes over me. "Wait," I call out, stepping around the bar so I can see her.

"Umm…" Shit, what was the point of that? "Hang out with me while I get ready?"

She turns around, a single eyebrow lifted high. "Y-you want to 'hang out' while you get ready?" A squeak spills out of her.

"Heh… Yep."

She leans against the wall and looks me up and down. Then she pushes off, shrugs, and steps forward. "Sure. Want me to hold your hand while you go potty, too?" She laughs and pokes me in the stomach, the creases in her tight features suddenly relaxed.

Aside from that jest, we head down the stairs without a word. In fact, the entire time I'm getting ready, neither of us say anything at all. She lies on her back, messing with her phone the whole time.

Something about it just feels right.

When I walk out of the adjoining bathroom after styling my hair, she rolls over to her belly and pushes up on her elbows to give me a once-over. "Handsome," she says, a true smile lighting up her eyes.

"Thanks." I return a smile of my own.

Knocking pulls our attention to the doorway. Porter leans there, forearm on the frame near his head. "You about to head out?" he asks.

"Yeah, man. I was just grabbing my wallet, protection, and keys. You ready?"

Movement from the bed catches my eye and distracts my focus away from Porter for a second. Remi had adjusted again, and her legs now dangle off the edge, her phone and hands in her lap as she watches our conversation.

"Almost," he answers. "You go ahead, though. I'll be right behind you. Gonna take care of a couple last minute account details here."

He looks from me to Remi and back again before he raps his knuckles on the doorframe and leaves.

"Account details?" Remi asks, her voice raised just above a whisper. The strange hitch in her breathy tone catches me as odd.

"Yeah, we're taking it digital. Scan and pay sort of deal."

Her eyes dart to the door and back to me again, fingers rubbing along the edges of her phone. "Don't you think that might risk leaving an electronic paper trail?"

I sit down and put my arm around her shoulders, glancing up at the doorway where Porter just stood. "Porter crossed all the *T*'s and dotted all the *I*'s," I answer. That same strange feeling that hit upstairs tugs hard on me again.

"Porter did. Of course. Always looking out for the company." She gives me one of those cute grimaces and chuckles under her breath, gaze falling to her lap.

I give her a little jostle. "Hey... um... look... I know you don't want to go. But be my plus one? Not for the business, but for me. This'll be the first big thing we've taken on without Dad's guidance, and I want my sister there. If you hate it, you can stay in the car the whole time. I'm not racing tonight."

I mean every bit of my request, but the main reason I want her to come with me is because I don't want to leave her here.

Alone...

...or otherwise.

CHAPTER TWENTY-SEVEN

Remi

J ude's request is sincere. Too sincere. He's pulling the guilt card and doesn't even realize it. But the offer works twofold for me. Before coming back, I'd set some boundaries and intend on sticking to them.

I only want to be here if Jude is here. In this shared residence, Jude is my only protection against Porter. I may have lied to Crow about possibly attending their meet, but I'm keeping true to my word about not looking back — to leave Porter stalled at the line.

If he is hanging around here to "take care of a couple last minute account details," then here is exactly where I don't want to be. Even if I don't want to go to the meet. Neither meet. I want out of this lie. Out of this standoff. Out of the business.

But I don't want out of Jude's life. If I were in his shoes, I would make the exact same request. Come with me. Give me some moral support.

He would never ever say no.

My gaze flits back to where Porter had been standing, and I let out a heavy sigh. I had come home confident with my new plan, but Porter is already complicating it. He so easily proved how difficult it would be to avoid him as long as I am living under this roof. Am I proud that he has whittled me down to this quaking, fearful woman? No.

If the spark of amusement in his cold eyes mixed with the occasional smug twitch of his lips is any indicator, he knows his actions have had that effect on me. To him, he is winning. And although I do feel ashamed of my fear, I refuse to continue letting him win.

Even the simplicity of having Jude's arm around my shoulder makes me feel safer than I had just moments ago when Porter was looming in the doorway.

By agreeing to support my brother, I can avoid staying behind with Porter. From the comfort of his car, I can still keep uninvolved. Jude and I both know that is unlikely, though. "Okay. Yeah… I'll go with you. Give me a few minutes to get ready?"

Jude squeezes me once more before letting go. I push off the bed and leave his room, only to turn around just past the open door and meet his eyes. "Hang out with me while I get ready?" I ask quietly.

Jude swallows hard, and his face blanches. I know the request is way out in left field — the whisper of uncertainty unlike me. But whatever this strange thing is between us right now, it buzzes in my veins. Based on Jude's expression, I'd say he feels it, too. Maybe it's one of those stages of grief things?

With a nod, he gets off the bed, collects his things, and we walk through the living room, up the stairs, and toward the hallway.

Surprise, surprise; Porter is leaning against the bar, waiting. His eyes dart past me toward Jude, and he straightens.

Jude's voice hits me from behind. "Shouldn't you be in the office? I'm good with you being late, bro, but not that late." Jude passes me and claps Porter on the shoulder, both men rigid and tense. "Now isn't the time to stand around."

While they're talking, I slide my phone into my clutch on the bar beside Porter, slip past them, and head to my room, not caring so much that Jude "hangs out" while I'm getting ready, but more that he is around when Porter is.

Clearly my asking him to accompany me was a good call. Porter follies, his voice becoming fainter as I distance myself from the conversation by making my way down the hallway. "Thought you'd be gone by now, too. Your empire awaits after all."

I can't help but roll my eyes, envisioning him bowing at the waist.

Jude speaks up. "Remi is riding with me. She decided to come. We'll head out as soon as she's ready."

The upper level becomes weighted with silence. I don't wait to hear what is said at that point. As soon as footsteps echo down the hall, I don't even bother to look back. I slip into my room. But this time, instead of closing the door, I keep it wide open. An invitation for Jude. A statement to Porter that I'm watching. On guard. He won't have the opportunity to linger outside my door without Jude or me knowing about it.

Sure enough, the footsteps stop roughly halfway down the hallway at about the point where he would turn to go into the office to take care of those supposed account details.

Ears perked for any noise, I scan my closet for an outfit. Jude's footsteps never come. But they never leave either. By my best guess, he's taken Porter's previous spot against the bar.

I wrench my head to the side and lean back a little to peek around the doorframe and check my assumption. My guess was wrong, though. Porter is still there, and across from the office, the bathroom door is closed.

Jude had followed me after all but made a pitstop. Porter pins me with a glare, calling me out on everything without saying a single word. Goosebumps and a sheen of sweat cover me from head to toe.

His elbow, forearm, and hand rest loosely on the bar top, fingers drumming a quiet pattern.

The bathroom door squeaks open, Jude steps out and heads back toward the kitchen where Porter still stands. Porter gives Jude a tight smile, pushes away from the bar, and passes him en route to the office.

"What do women usually wear to these things?" I pitch my voice, snapping Jude's attention away from Porter.

Jude chuckles, leaning against the bar. "Something sexy, usually. Wear whatever, though.

Hell, if you plan on staying in the car anyway, you can just keep the sweats on."

I roll my eyes at him. He knows damn well that if I'm there for support, I need to dress the part. Since I'm not riding my bike, I have a lot more shoe options. I decide on heels. That's about as sexy as I'm willing to take it. Form fitting black jeans, black heels, and my favorite leather jacket.

After a quick finger brush of my hair, I grab a few basic makeup items with the intention of touching up my face while we drive, clack down the hallway, snatch my clutch off the bar, and follow Jude out.

CHAPTER TWENTY-EIGHT

A s soon as my ass hits Jude's creamy leather bucket seats, the weight of what's going on settles, and guilt slams into me; Revelry had invited me well before Jude did. Well, kind of. Technically, I was grandfathered in to tonight's meet the day I was born.

That mental thought carries over aloud as Jude gets behind the wheel. "Speaking of which… Do you guys have a crew name, yet?"

"Of course," he responds. "Just got the decals in today."

Twisting around, I search for the gawky sticker I definitely didn't notice prior to getting in.

"Bottom left of the driver's window. They keep them low-key in this area. Figured we wouldn't reinvent that wheel," Jude assists. "Midnight Runners."

"Nice. I like it."

"Thanks."

To distract myself from the uncomfortable silence that follows, as soon as we stop at the first light, I flip down the mirrored visor, line up the makeup items in my lap, and get to work dabbing on concealer and a little setting powder for that fading bruise. I was never the greatest at doing the winged-liner thing but somehow manage to do pretty darn good this time.

The light turns green, but Jude waits for me to finish applying some mascara and a bit of blush and putting everything away before moving forward. "Guess you're not staying in the car?" he chuckles.

"Knowing I have that option as a fallback helps." I give a soft smile. "But, no. I'm not going to support you from inside a vehicle."

His eyes scan my now-tidied face. "The makeup makes you look older."

"Older good? Or older bad?"

Jude shrugs. "Both."

My eyes pop wide, and he grins.

"You're grown up is all. Makes my chest feel tight and shit sometimes. The makeup doesn't help."

"Hate to break it to ya, bro, but I've been wearing makeup for several years now. When I'm not riding, of course."

"Yeah, I know. Guess it's just different now. You're beautiful instead of cute."

My cheeks burn redder than the blush I had put on. "Stop. You're making me feel all weird and awkward."

Jude's cheeks lift, and his eyes crinkle in the corners, the dark-brown of his irises highlighted with a spark of yellow as we approach the next light and it changes.

"Well, you're not too bad yourself there sport. Especially with that suave five o'clock shadow you pull off so well. Makes you look like a man finally. Took ya a while."

He finishes shifting to neutral and applying the handbrake and narrows a playful glare at me. Something catches his eye over my shoulder, and his line of sight adjusts. A small smile twitches on his lips. Keeping my focus on him, with a hint of my own smile, I state, "Oh… Say it isn't so…"

His twitch turns into a full-blown, handsome grin. With a groan, I look out my window. As expected, a car enthusiast is foaming at the mouth, indicating for us to roll the window down.

Racking my mind, I try to remember where I've spotted the car. I don't have to track too far back, seeing as this whirlwind didn't start too terribly long ago: the time I had seen it — assuming this is the same one — was the night I met Trenton and Hayes. A red Trans Am was entering the parking lot of The Crowbar and Grill just as I was peddling away.

"This is why I never ride with you anywhere. Takes twice the time to get places between traffic-light bonding and running digs on every straight. Does someone seriously challenge you every time you stop?"

Jude's competitor is young, eagerly revving the engine as Jude slides down my window using the controls on his side. "Only the ones who don't know better."

"You aren't seriously—"

"Oh… shit…" The boy's awestruck voice travels across lanes. "Was not expecting a right-hand driver. So… uh… is it fast?" he yells past me at Jude.

My head falls back against the seat. I tilt it to the side toward Jude and roll my eyes at him.

Jude smothers a laugh with his fist. Instead of answering the question with words, he revs. The engine purrs beautifully. "Aw, don't give me that look. I feel bad for the poor kid," he whispers through tight teeth, smiling and nodding at his opponent in agreement. "This is a prime opportunity to teach him a lesson. Gotta be a good role model, after all. Just spreading the knowledge, Remi. All for the greater good."

The time for chatting is dwindling. Jude molds into his seat, releases the handbrake, loops his fingers under the gear knob's lockout lever, and shifts into first.

This car earned its infamous nickname Godzilla for a reason. In a normal driving situation, she just wants to go. The effort is minimal. Ripping the asphalt is what she was designed to do. Period.

My focus trails from Jude to the stale red light then to the other driver. His hands open and close repeatedly over the wheel, teeth worrying at his bottom lip.

No one is around. The road is empty. This is what racers' wet dreams are made of. His excitement and nervousness is so energy-rich, I can sense it thrum in my own body.

The crossing traffic light turns yellow, and Jude waits a short moment. A blink before our light turns, he roars the engine to life. But when the green blazes, Jude throws me a wink and, out of the kindness of his generous heart, gives the red Trans Am the jump. That kindness only lasts an exhalation of breath, though.

On the next inhale my heart goes from fully functioning to stopping completely as he launches ahead. Only to jumpstart when Jude shifts again, and my body propels forward and slams back against the seat.

The road, signs, and lights are all indiscernible blurs, but the red streak Jude passes is unmistakable.

In all of five seconds or so, the race is over — a bump of feel-good with a high that will last hours for Jude's new admirer.

"Throw the hazards for me, Rem." Jude's voice bubbles with laughter as he lets off the gas.

I reach over and turn on the hazard lights, helping Jude claim his win. When the red Trans Am paces us, I turn them back off.

Jude salutes him, and the kid flashes a goofy, lopsided grin before falling back and pulling behind us.

A giddy chuckle betrays my attempt at impassiveness. "Never in my life have I ever seen anyone so happy to lose."

"Making dreams come true — how's that for a real estate tagline?" Jude jokes. When his adrenaline-glassed eyes meet mine and he gives me a toothy grin, my heart is nearly captured by the wind whooshing in through the open windows and carried off into the night.

The moment is bittersweet. This light, joyful banter between us is something I have dearly missed.

Jude's ensuing laugh trails, though, and the cheerful sound mixes with everything but happiness. He clears his throat. "Do you still trust me?" he asks. "I mean, we're still tight, right? Can tell each other anything?"

The seat belt tightens on my hip as I turn to face him. "Is that why you wanted me to come with you tonight?" I ask. Both anger and anxiousness braid around the question.

His fingers tighten over the steering wheel. "Maybe. Part of the reason."

I press my lips together and huff out a breath from my nose. "Yeah... I still trust you. But as you said, I'm grown now; there comes a time when a line has to be drawn to divide just, exactly, how much information you tell your big brother."

"Fair enough," he responds, fingers tapping. "Something is bothering me, though. I'm worried about you, Remi."

My anger softens, but the anxiety blooms. I slash a hand through the air. "Ah, don't worry about me. You have enough on your plate."

"Too much," he mumbles under his breath before clearing his throat and bluntly asking, "How involved are you with the Revelry crew?"

Just like that, the anger returns… and it brings friends this time. Conflicting emotions rave inside me at once — all neon glow sticks and thumping bass.

However, I see no sense in lying about my budding relationships with Crow, Hayes, and Trenton. What would be the point? Porter already knows something is up between us. Clearly he had said something to Jude…

"Personally, very involved. Automotively, I want to be a part of Revelry about as much as I want to be a part of Midnight Runners, which is not at all in case you hadn't picked up on my not-so-subtle hints. A semester out of school is all I promised — to organize our new life… To grieve. That promise didn't include an active position in the business."

Jude nods, and his fingers stop tapping. His eyes leave the road for a heartbeat, flicking toward me before turning to the road again. "If it's one of them leaving marks on you, I'll fucking kill them, Remi. I'm not playing."

My shoulders tense, and I face forward in the seat again. The anxiety and concern inside me gathers and congeals. I work my mind for a response — the right response — but there isn't one. Telling the truth would be preferable; however, my stomach twists and vision teases black at the edges at the thought. Clearly, I still have some leveling up to do.

The moment Jude learns about Porter and me, our lives will change forever. That built trust. The ease of our conversations. Our relationship. Everything.

Unfortunately, my silence only serves to worsen Jude's rising suspicions. His hand unclenches from the wheel, and he slams his open palm against it.

I jolt at the sudden aggression — the hair on my arms rises at the volatile energy pulsing in the vehicle. I move my mouth and lift my tongue to form the words in the guys' defense, but realize in doing so, it will only lead to another question, and another,

and another. In turn, more lies. More excuses. Or…
More silence.

Silence. Silence is the lesser of the evils, I decide.

Jude is smart. Distracted by grief and business lately, but super smart. The gears are turning. He's putting pieces together. One day soon, hopefully, he will figure everything out on his own. I pray that day comes, even despite the potential consequences.

Because if Jude figures it out on his own due to Porter getting sloppy, then Porter can't place blame on me. Perhaps then, he will continue to keep my much bigger secret safe. The one that can never be unearthed no matter how this crew and club stuff unravels.

Taking a vow of silence is a reach. But it's the only thread I can grasp right now.

Thread.

The word has me glancing down at my fingers. Miraculously, the ring Trenton had given me is still there. A symbol of my hope. A symbol of my integrity. A symbol of everything I am right now…

…Barely hanging on.

CHAPTER TWENTY-NINE

J ude's temper lingers, riding along as a silent, formidable passenger in the confines of his car. Fortunately, he doesn't press for any more details, though.

Jittery from the race and the building pressure of everything going on and already eager to get this night over with, I stare aimlessly at the road ahead, tracking each turn.

The unease flowing through me rushes faster the farther we drive. This route is familiar.

I twist my fingers as Jude leads us toward Steel Field Road — the same area where Crow had taken me — turn for turn. Knowing the dates fall on the same night is bad enough. Please don't let it be at the same location, too.

Earlier, when Jude was getting ready, I had sent the guys a group text — much to Crow's dismay — letting them know that I was staying home. I didn't reveal in exact terms that I knew and remembered their meet was tonight, but I threw out a couple hints — wishing them a good evening and telling them to be safe.

That was when I still planned on staying home, of course.

With shaky hands, I unzip my clutch and dig for my phone and the golden ticket.

My fingers graze against one but not the other. Heart racing, I spread the clutch open wide and begin to frantically scan the limited contents.

Revelry's golden ticket stands out among the items, but my phone is gone, despite me having put it in there before changing clothes.

Panicking, I study the invitation's coordinates before turning my attention to the aftermarket navigation screen in Jude's car. Without permission, I tap on the display until it shows coordinate numbers rather than street names — the coordinates are different.

Relief flushes through me, and I return the nav back to its original map.

"We're not doing the takeover tonight. Our meet is separate from theirs," Jude explains, noticing my somewhat manic behavior and coming to a correct assumption. "A statement. A threat. Proving to them our sway is stronger than they likely realize. That's what this meet is all about."

I attempt to swallow the boulder of air lodged in my throat, but it remains there, thick and obtrusive. My fingers itch to text them that my plans had changed for the night and why. This lie was never intentional.

As my only way of keeping the playing field even without losing the trust of either side, I never planned on telling either crew about the exacts regarding each meet. Nor did I plan to attend. Both moves seemed fair. But now, with no way of updating Revelry, I feel like even more of a traitor than before. Imagine that.

Keeping my involvement with the Midnight Runners a secret came with the job assignment. There are plenty of occupations out there that require confidentiality. Only when my heart betrayed me did the confidentiality cross a line. Only then did my secrecy begin to feel like betrayal. But I had started coming to terms with that and manipulated the job's execution in my favor. In everyone's favor. By staying involved with the people on both sides but excluding myself from "business" matters, I could coast for a while.

My personal relationships, whether it be with my brother or my… boyfriends?… those are neither parties' affairs where the other relationship is concerned.

I had tried to leave the situation with Porter entirely separate, too — its own entity — but both Jude and Revelry made that incredibly difficult to accomplish.

When Jude parks, the red Trans Am is still behind us. Jude and I share a glance, coming to the same conclusion: since this is a meet and this kid clearly likes to race, he was likely headed here just like we were. He parks in front of us, hops out, and leans against the side of his car, hand visored over his eyes to block out Jude's headlights.

We exit the vehicle and walk straight over to him. Jude extends a hand, and the two clasp at the forearm. "Fancy seeing you here. Sick Skyline. You running her tonight?"

"GT-R. Skylines are what grandmas drive. Gotta specify if you want to be a proper gearhead," Jude explains, taking the kid under his wing, like the great role model he is. "And, nah, I'm not racing. If I run, no one has a chance at the pot."

The kid snorts, his features lax and eyes bloodshot — high as a damn kite. "Thanks for looking out for the lesser of us then. Name's Boyd, by the way." He digs into his pocket, pulls out a piece of paper. One that gleams yellow in the glow of Jude's headlights.

Before Jude can grab it, I steal the shiny paper and twist it into the light. A golden ticket. Same date, time, and place as the one Crow gave me.

The ticket crushes as I curl my fingers around it and shoot a glare at Jude. Jude jerks his head to the side, indicating he'd like to talk to me away from his paycheck.

I toss the golden ticket at him, both in frustration and because he's my brother.

His hand comes to the back of his head, and he rubs it gently. "Did you just… throw that at me?" he laughs, turning around to face me, outside of the spotlight created by his headlights. "I told you, we're proving sway. The entire county is invited. If they bring a golden ticket with them, Porter and I match their down payment."

"You mean if they stand up the Revelry meet."

"Exactly. Money speaks, Remi. You know it does. If Revelry thought that people would be loyal to them simply because they have location seniority, they're about to be grossly disappointed."

My lips press together, and I cross my arms. Jude matches me, temper for temper. Except amusement twinkles in his eyes, whereas frustration clouds mine.

CHAPTER THIRTY

Using my hands as an improvised megaphone, I make a friendly announcement to the racers and spectators congregating: "Looks like the turnout is going to be small tonight, folks!"

"Is this supposed to be a cash event?" one of the guys from Flo-Riders hollers back.

Part of the suspense of showing up to our Golden Ticket events is finding out if we're laying bets. Since that's on a need-to-know-basis, we don't announce cash events until the meet starts. Prevents word from spreading too soon or to the wrong people.

Regardless, every Golden Ticket event is highly anticipated and generally lasts until the sun begins to rise. Bigger and better than the subclass meets.

"Not tonight," I respond. "Soon, though, and it'll be epic. How does everyone feel about a good 'ol three-course Dine and Dash on this lovely

238

evening?" I ask, pivoting in a small circle so my voice disperses.

Those close by whoop in agreement. Those who aren't listening or can't hear because of the racket of vehicles and conversation begin getting the news old-school, telephone-game style. "Since Mama isn't here tonight to teach us proper dining etiquette, we'll start with dessert," I continue.

"What if we don't like donuts?" a youngster scoffs in the distance, spouting shit as usual.

"Well, kid, if a banana split is more your thing, who am I to judge? I personally favor that creamy glaze and tight little hole in the center, though, and I'm the one creating the menu." A certain creamy, tight hole having nothing to do with donuts comes to mind, and my cock struggles to decide which state of performance is preferable — that of being rock hard at the thought of having been inside her or flaccid at the thought of possible heartbreak and deception.

The area fills with laughter. Revving up the attendees now accomplished, I give them tonight's specials as the process demands: field donuts for dessert here near the county line, drifting as an appetizer at a recently-closed grocery store in the neighboring county, and digs as the main course back in this jurisdiction on our favored back-country road.

Spiel in the rearview, I turn to Crow and Hayes, my spokesman buzz waning in an instant at the sight of their dour expressions. Hayes palms the back of his neck and shoves the other hand into his pocket. We've never had this small of a turnout, even back in the day when The Gulf Coasters first launched.

Crow drags a hand across his mouth. Instead of dropping it, though, he lifts a pointed finger and waggles it at both me and Hayes. "Remi has something to do with this," he says matter-of-factly.

"Remi. Right. The girl who has spent every day and night with us for the past few days — not to mention a good bit of time before that — somehow managed to convince more than half the crews in a tri-county area to ditch a Golden Ticket event." I roll my eyes at him. "Wake the fuck up, Crow. Time to start trusting people again."

Hell, I hope I'm not wrong; I want to remind him that it has been three years since his — our — ability to trust people disintegrated, but he wears the reminder every day. I, on the other hand, didn't need to trust Remi in order to sleep with her. But, in the same lane, that's how this all started. Now, my body, heart, and mind are doing more than just getting a quick release.

I shoot a pleading look at Hayes for backup, but his eyes drop and that hand rubs tighter against the back of his neck. A flicker of movement has my focus adjusting — his fingers twitching to tap inside his jeans' pocket. I throw my head back with a growl of frustration. "You too?"

Hayes's head remains tilted down, but his gaze lifts over his glasses.

Then…

…Then, he shrugs.

"Seriously!? Riddle me that," I huff. The conversation Hayes and I had earlier today about that message from the mysterious DoubleD doesn't help my sputtering heart.

Hayes releases a heavy breath and straightens, but he doesn't have anything else to say. I pull out my phone and shoot Remi a text, ready to prove them wrong. Ready to cure the acidic unsettling in my stomach.

Her last message already explained that she was staying home tonight. I was kinda glad, honestly. Not because I didn't want her here, but because if she seemed less than interested, then maybe Crow would get off her damn back.

Show too much interest, and his hackles would remain raised. Or so I thought. Seems those damn hackles refuse to go down regardless.

Me: *Hey, pet. About to hit the tarmac. Thinking about you, wish you were here as a good luck charm.*

Crow snoops over my shoulder before I press send. "Pet?" He scoffs, spins on his heels, and throws his hands up in the air.

I launch forward and punch him on the arm. "Fuck you, Dark Cloud. Inside joke? You know, har har?"

Crow tenses, fingers curling into his palms. "It would do you a bit of damn good to take off those rose-colored glasses you've been catwalking in. Rose isn't really your color."

"At least it's not fucking black. You told Hayes what you told me yet?"

If Crow's eyes narrow any further they'll cross. A warning? So… does that mean he didn't tell Hayes about his obsession with Remi yet?

Hypocrite.

"We're at a meet, and all you can do is fucking think, breathe, and talk about her," Crow growls. "Keep it up, and I'm taking your keys. You're not racing when consumed the way you are. At least I can keep my feelings in check."

The au-fucking-dacity of his comment. Oh, my feelings are in check. If they weren't I'd have followed her ass home and nipped at her heels until she left. Porter wouldn't have had a chance to so much as look at her without me baring teeth and snapping like a rabid animal. Wearing those so-called rose-colored glasses Crow mentioned is the most effective medicine for the sickness inside me. Well… that and copious, mindless sex.

He knows that.

But even if, on the off-fucking-chance there is truth in his words, it pisses me off that he is calling me out when he has no room to speak. "No, see that's just the thing. *You* are not keeping *your* feelings in check. Not at all. If anyone needs their keys tabled…"

The only thing that prevents Crow and I from bumping chests is the approach of a panting, wild-eyed crew leader. "One of my guys just called with some news I think you might find interesting." The three of us turn our rapt attention to him. "They're accepting golden tickets as partial DP. Tonight. Right now."

"Their meet is running the same time as ours?" Crow asks, raising a smug brow at me rather than directing the question at the guy.

"The numbers are excellent. Payout even better. The leaders match every ticket holder's DP, doubling the pot. My crew is fired up. They want to crash the even—"

"No," Crow interjects, the smugness of his features flattening. "That's probably what they expect us to do. I'm not putting everyone at risk by feeding into some infant crew's concept of how shit around here works. Let them get stupid. We don't run that way. On your way back to your crew, go ahead and spread the news that if anyone else has any wild ideas, they can see themselves out for good."

News — whichever the leader decided to share — begins spreading like fire. A match tossed to a line of fuel. We stand and quietly watch while more crews leave to either cause shit with this new street racing club or to join them.

Crow rubs a hand down his face and when his expression is visible again, all the aggression is gone, replaced by anxiety and dejection.

Our argument becomes unimportant, and I scramble to lift him up — to stop him from unhinging. "Look man. The black and whites know we're out here tonight. They're turning a blind eye, as usual. They find a meet anywhere else, and they'll take 'em down. Let the law do their job."

"That is *if* the law does its job," he says, defeated. "You know as well as I do, none of us are making the call."

Right. Unspoken street racing rule. No matter the crew or club, you just don't do that shit.

I turn to Hayes. "You're awfully quiet."

Hayes clears his throat. "Yeah… Later, man. Let's give those who stayed what they came for. At the end of the Dine and Dash, the ones proving loyalty are most deserving of receiving their meal receipt anyway."

The weight of the new stack of golden tickets weighs heavy in my pocket, but not as heavy as the vow of silence both Crow and Hayes have taken. This mediator position is uncomfortable. Hayes has clearly decided to not share the details of DoubleD's tip off. Crow… well… he's still refusing to openly admit his feelings for Remi.

The crash happened three years ago, and while no amount of time will take it away, the fact that we're still dealing with the repercussions doesn't help either. Eventually he needs to bounce back, though. I am more than ready; I just wish he was, too.

Limbs shaking with adrenaline-fueled frustration, I give each of my best friends a separate, supportive nod. "Well, if this conversation is over… let us dine."

"I'm out," Crow says, shocking the shit out of the both of us.

"You've never missed a meet. Not since—"

"I'm out," he stresses. "You guys got this. I need a drink." Hayes and I share a look. Crow follows that look. "Stay. You follow me and we're gonna have problems."

I hold my hands up, palms out. "Fine."

Hayes doesn't seem so sure, though. But a threatening glare from Crow sets him straight. He holds his hands up in defense, too. "Okay, man. We'll text you."

Crow gives us a sharp nod and leaves. As soon as he is in his car and is at least a quarter mile away, I pull my phone back out to check for a response from Remi.

"Anything?" Hayes asks.

"Nope."

A long-time buried fury begins simmering in the crevices of my veins... and Hayes choosing to keep quiet about whatever new information he's privy to only serves to infiltrate each crack.

CHAPTER THIRTY-ONE

Remi

Since this is the first large-scale meet I have ever attended, I have no experiences to compare it against. Sure, I've been a bystander at the occasional, small meet back in California, but that's about it; I've never participated in or worked a meet before. The street is packed. Cars line both sides of the road for what seems like miles, or at least as far into the distance as I can see. Some people even maneuvered toward the trees.

Jude's wide-eyed expression proves he wasn't expecting this big of a turnout. With a little help from me, because I hate seeing the damn shitstorm that is forming from the lack of organization — and because I have an increasing thirst for knowledge — I established a toll area at the front, bluntly refusing to engage in tonight's festivities aside from that.

The setup is enough for him to collect tickets and receive payment from participants and attendees alike via the digital QR system Porter had designed.

With this much activity, it'd be a damn miracle if the cops don't get tipped. All it would take is a single, non-participant rolling through trying to get from point A to point B and realizing something blatantly fishy is going on.

My ingenious brother comes up with a backup idea, though: if someone random comes through, he simply explains there's a big employee event going on at the local waste management company down the road. At midnight.

But, hey, whatever. I promised myself not to get too involved. I do, however, stay at the faux toll booth as moral support. Every five cars or so, Jude curses Porter under his breath.

"Well, hey," I mention, "on the bright side, whatever last minute account stuff he had to take care of must've worked." I roll my eyes behind Jude's back, figuring damn well that Porter had no intention of sticking behind for account purposes.

Porter probably intended on staying behind to harass me. Thankfully, his plans were thwarted by whatever Jude's intuition was telling him at the time. Because, yeah, I don't think he encouraged me to go with him just to ask about my involvement with Crow, Hayes, and Trenton.

With Porter not here, though, and none of these people familiar with Jude, he will need help if Porter doesn't hurry and show. Otherwise, he'll end up looking like an inexperienced asshole out here.

Tons of vehicles roll up — trucks, SUVs, sports cars, sedans; you name it, someone shows up driving one. The organizational freak in me cringes at the thought of how he's going to manage this. Organize the best races. Track the wins.

I know for a fact he has never done it before. Been a participant? Yes. Been in charge of street races, though? No. Especially one that has garnered this much attention.

The road is two lanes, one going east and one going west. That's it. One race will run at a time, and everything continues until the cops show up, all the matchups on the roster have been raced, or the sun begins to rise.

At least with this new digital plan, no one will have to stick around to wait for their earnings, because with an event this size, the cops will undoubtedly show up well before the races are complete. If things go south, they can make refunds with the press of a button. Same goes with divvying funds to winners. All the money is funneled through

Lance Industries, and compared to the usual cash-flow of the company, tonight's is mere pennies. Nothing flashy. Guess I can see the strategy behind this electronic process.

Go big, or go home, right?

And we sure as hell don't want to go home.

Makes me wonder, though. Are The Gulf Coasters organized as an established business to help with the flow of cash accumulated from their meets? And, if so, where does their legal funding come from?

Ad revenue from their forum comes to mind, of course.

Something to inquire about when we are all a bit cozier, perhaps.

Jude looks down at his watch and rolls his shoulders. "Shit… I can't believe I'm actually saying this, but we're gonna have to cap it. I can't sit here all night."

There's a hopeful suggestion in those words, but I don't humor the nudge. Instead, I stand up, fold the camping chair someone had so kindly offered me, and tuck it under my arm. "Yeah, good luck with that part, bro."

I start down the street, walking the center road markings, while Jude wraps everything up. My path ends at two cars lined up — A Chevelle in the east-bound traffic lane and a Maverick in the west-bound lane. Members are speaking to the racers through their windows, and spectators alternate glances from the cars to their phones, typing in wagers.

A random person rushes up to me and asks, "Hey, you flagging?" Since most of the attendees saw me sitting behind Jude at our makeshift booth, they likely assume I'm helping run things.

"N—"

"Yep, she's your girl." A familiar voice cuts me off from behind. I spin toward the sound, nearly dropping the borrowed chair.

Porter.

I stagger backward, so accustomed to my flight instinct kicking in anytime he gets near me at this point. Noting that there are a lot of people around and there is safety in numbers, I clasp my hand over my chest and take in a shaky breath. "Shit, you scared me." A breathy, recovery chuckle trickles from my trembling lips as I dart a glance over my shoulder at the guy who was asking the question. Returning my attention to Porter, I state, "Jude and I had an arrangement. I'm only here for moral support."

Once again, I underestimated Porter; he steps up to me, not caring about our audience, removes the chair from under my arm, and tosses it to the grass on the side of the road. It slides toward someone's feet, and they have to jump back to avoid getting hit. "What the fuck?" the spectator grumbles.

Porter doesn't give a damn. He does, however, treat me more gently than when we are behind closed doors; his hand slips under the hair behind my ear and snakes to the back of my head. I stand stock-still so as not to draw any extra attention. Then, his finger depresses a soft spot at the base of my skull, and a dull throb twinges my nerves, causing my knees to buckle. "Line the cars up, Remi. Or, when the cops show tonight, someone might just tip them off about what really happened on the port. Not too sure how Jude would feel about watching his baby sister be taken away in the back of a cop car on the same night he finds out she is the reason their father died, but I can take a guess."

My chest collapses in on itself, cutting off my air supply. The words attack my gut worse than

Porter's knee did during our last rendezvous. My knees buckle further and eyes water due to the ache running down my spine and the injustice of the entire situation.

When he lets go, simply slipping his hand down the side of my neck and over my shoulder as if caressing a lover, it takes every bit of my remaining energy to keep from crumbling onto the asphalt.

CHAPTER THIRTY-TWO

T wo minutes too late, Jude approaches behind him. "About damn time," he accuses Porter. "Chill out. I saw what you were doing at the front, so I went around and started signing up people on the east side. Put up markers, assigned stewards, and sprayed for mosquitoes on the way back, too. Road is prepped for the first race."

My mouth parts on a silent gasp. Porter is quite possibly the most talented manipulator I have ever known. I can't believe I'm just now noticing it, too. Guess when you've known someone for so long, you become blind to the manipulation that undulates under the surface of their facade. Kind of like that one spot in your house where you put things down when you first enter — a table top, counter, or something along those lines. Eventually, as things start to collect, you no longer really "see" the mess.

As if providing the perfect example of this blindness raw and in-person, Jude blinks at him, biting down on the bait at the exact moment Porter yanks the damn line to set the hook. "Oh. Well, shit.

I thought you ditched me for some pussy or something."

"Not for a lack of trying," Porter answers, daring the quickest of glances in my direction. My focus glazes as I stare at him dumbly. A repulsive shiver sweeps over me.

More than eager to distance myself from the situation, for more than one reason at this point, I turn to the guy who had asked about the racers being lined up. Throughout mine and Porter's exchange, he had been hanging out behind us, patiently waiting for a legit answer to the question he had asked.

While Jude and Porter huddle in continued conversation, I scan the roadside and the groups of people standing around and talking. The air buzzes with anxiousness and excitement, everyone having waited long enough while things got arranged.

I address the guy. "Yeah, I'll signal." The offer comes out as a sigh of defeat. Before I step away from Jude and Porter to get started, I shoot a question to Jude over my shoulder: "You have some sort of roster tonight? These guys set?"

Both Jude and Porter pull out their phones. Once they find the information, they both lift their heads and look toward the two cars that are lined up. "Yeah, they're first up," Jude responds.

He moves forward toward the cars, but Porter pulls him back. "Remi will take care of it."

Jude's eyes drop to where Porter has him gripped, and Porter lets go, shoving that same hand into his pocket. Jude's eyes snap to me. "You changed your mind?"

My eyes flick from Jude to Porter and back again. "Heh, yeah… I guess. Unless you don't want me to flag?"

Jude shakes his head, a smile spreading across his face. With a single clap, he swoops forward, crushes me in his arms, and spins me around. "Hell yeah!" He gives me a big kiss on the cheek and lets go.

As the undeserving recipient of his pride and excitement, a shaky breath does the rounds through me from nose to lungs and back again before I am able to plaster on a fake smile. I wish he could sense — feel — the churning in my stomach and the heavy weight of guilt and dread in my limbs. I wish he could get inside my mind and extract everything I keep locked tight.

"Got your phone?" Jude asks.

I shake my head. "No. It wasn't in my clutch when we were driving here. Guess I left it in your room."

Porter lifts his phone, swipes the screen on, and holds it out to me. "You hang on to this. If Jude or I need anything, we'll text from his phone." He then points at an app screen, the one similar to what we were using to accept payments. "Everyone participating tonight scanned the QR code that led them to this app. They can register their vehicles, include mods and any other important specs using the app, and then it populates the races." His finger flicks right to left again and again to show me the order of races.

Eyes wide, I nod.

Damn, this is impressive.

My eyes flutter, close to flicking up to look at his face — the mastermind behind the design, no doubt. But I blink the temptation away, accepting his phone and memorizing the first few races before forcing it into my pocket.

Jude pats me on the back and jogs off toward his car, holding up a finger and yelling over his shoulder, "Give me a few minutes more before you signal the drivers."

In order to inform the closest circle of onlookers that we're making forward progress, I go ahead and step toward the first two racers, walking the center line between each vehicle and stopping at the front windows.

Being between two older domestics, my mind flashes with memories of Trenton, and my heart does a little twist. Is he lined up right now? Who will he race? Will he win?

Seeing as I'm at a race anyway, despite not wanting to attend one, I wish I had gone to Revelry's event after all. I wish I hadn't even left their house, even if doing so made absolutely perfect sense at the time.

I bend down and look at each racer, giving them a smile. One thing I most certainly got from my father was his affable friendliness, even on the bad days. "Just because you're having a bad day, doesn't mean everyone around you needs to suffer too," he would always say, lifting my lips up, pinched between his thumb and forefinger.

After flashing that similar friendly grin at each driver, I let them know it'll just be a few more minutes but that I will go ahead and line them up.

I stand and find my spot out in front of them. The Chevelle is just a foot or so too far back, so I point at him, wait for his acknowledgement, then curl my fingers toward me. He inches forward until I signal him by holding a fist up. When everything looks good I give both guys a quick nod.

The racers' partners jog forward, at the ready to dump or spray sticky juice on the road in front of the back tires to help with traction.

"Spraying for mosquitoes" as Porter had mentioned earlier. Too bad they didn't spray for actual mosquitoes; this muggy heat and the nearby damp forest of trees is prime habitat.

By the time the racers are straight, Jude is back, megaphone in hand, and the screech of a connection squeals over the conversations and rumble of engines.

The area quiets down a little, but not much. With a crowd this large and distractions everywhere, getting everyone's undivided attention is impossible. Jude presses the siren in one more quick attempt to shift the crowd's focus.

He welcomes everyone to the meet, introduces himself, and thanks them for coming. "Everyone here who has access to the app should know the rules specific to this meet. Of course, most etiquette is common sense and unspoken. If you aren't interested in sticking to the straight and narrow, go ahead and leave. You fuck up tonight, I can promise you won't be racing through this club ever again."

From there, he simply tells everyone to have a good time, be safe, and that any payouts will be sent within twenty-four hours.

Porter quickly snatches the megaphone and adds, "This part isn't on the app, but listen closely: the beautiful woman flagging racers tonight is Jude's sister. There is a strict, no-touching policy. And if you get squirrely off the line and she ends up getting hurt flagging you fuckers in, spending your life in prison will be the least of your worries."

My eyes shoot wide before narrowing playfully at both Porter and Jude. Onlookers chuckle. Jude included. Jude claps Porter on the shoulder in thanks, steals the megaphone back and says, "Let's burn some rubber!"

CHAPTER THIRTY-THREE

Crow

Nobody bothered to share where the rival crew had set up tonight. Not that I stuck around long enough to investigate; time waits for no one, after all.

Instead, inquiries took place over the phone as I drove manically through town and back toward the beach side to my apartment so I could swap vehicles.

After a few phone calls to the right people, I found their location; it just had to be Steel Field. Where I had taken Remi just the other night. Talk about an uncanny coincidence.

Yeah-fucking-right.

Since everyone who is anyone knows who the Supra's driver is, I loop around to the house's attached garage and grab an alternative — one that local racers haven't seen on the road in a few years and shouldn't bat an eyelash at if they catch a glimpse of it tonight. My intention, though, is to stay out of sight, anyway. One can never be too careful.

Hopping into the Caddy V coupe, I try hard not to let my focus drift to its mangled garage-mate. The automatic garage door opens painstakingly slow while I buckle up and turn her on, challenging my poor discipline; my eyes catch on the twisted bumper and busted glass of the 'Lac CTS beside me.

As soon as the door is high enough for me to fit under, I peel out of there, forcing my eyes to stay open and focused on leaving the driveway without running into anything rather than pinch closed at the sight.

Taking a well-known backwoods cutoff after the East River that ends right at the center of the main straight on Steel Field Road, I drive straight toward a game of chicken with the woman threatening to be the rest of my undoing.

I park a ways inside the dense wildlife management area and cover the rest by foot. Closing the distance, I fight against the bumper-to-bumper traffic taking place in my damn head: I want Remi to be here because I'm right and she's been playing us, but... I want to be wrong. Fuck, I've never wanted to be more wrong in my life.

Please let me be wrong.

Trenton — the fucking asshole — called me out that night Remi and were at the bar after she showed up at my place vulnerable and silently screaming for help. Broken. Just like me.

I knew as soon as I touched her for the first time that she was the girl meant to be the glue that would bind me back together. But I also knew it would come at a great cost. That sour and curdling gut intuition glugged thicker than the blood pulsing through my cock, though.

I had hoped she would just go away — a one night stand like all the other girls Trenton and Hayes pick up. But she was so much more.

The fucking perfect piece to our incomplete puzzle. The woman none of us have — but all of us need — wrapped up in a single, perfect package.

That's why, when I spot her standing between two cars revving to race, a smile on her beautiful face, my heart rusts and crumbles.

Instead of simply recording on my phone, this time, I start a video meeting with Trenton and Hayes, knowing based on the time that they're likely done with dessert and are hopping to the next course.

If I have to see this shit, they have to see it, too. As soon as Hayes connects the call, I don't bother to wait or ask for T-Top before focusing the lens on Remi and recording the meeting to show Trenton a playback if he can't see this shit live.

She points to each car, lifts her arms, and drops them. As the cars launch past the starting line, she spins on her heels. The wind whips her hair over her shoulders and covers her face.

Her fingers come up to brush the strands away as she turns back around. In tight, black pants and hooker-spiked heels, she is dressed to fucking impress. Still smiling. Still trying to turn the engine that is my heart only for it to fucking stutter and grind.

Only when she complacently sits down in a camp chair at the edge of the woods do all my senses come rushing back. The twist of my heart is replaced with the pummeling of rage and hate.

I. Fucking. Knew. It. And that's the only reason why I'm not stumbling off in the opposite direction to suck in the breaths she just stole from my lungs.

Before I can change my mind, I shove the still recording phone into my pocket, bound out of the trees, and wrap a hand around her wrist. Pure animosity and fury course through me to the point that I can't even see straight. Dragging her into the woods, all I can picture is the girl who gifted me a coffee mug and stole my fucking heart while wearing a deceitful mask, and taking down the guys, the club — everyone who are my family — in the process.

She screeches in fear, but the sound of the next two cars burning out to heat their tires muffles her terror. I fling her around and press her against a tree, my palm covering her mouth.

Her dark-brown eyes blacken with rage, challenging me, and she wriggles under my hold. Chest heaving, eyes tracking all over her face, a new type of animosity courses through me, one that unfairly reminds me I am not the only person she is betraying.

Hand still clasped over her mouth, my knee and hip now pinning her against the tree, I dig into my pocket and pull out the phone. After verifying the live video is still running and both Trenton and Hayes are paying attention, I flip it around and shove it toward her, holding it far enough away so that she is able to see their faces — how much her actions will break my best friends.

She blinks rapidly as her eyes slowly focus on the screen. The moment she understands what she's looking at — that I caught proof of her betrayal on camera — her body turns to jelly.

No longer do Trenton and Hayes have to hear it from me; they get to see it in live action.

Her head shakes side to side, eyebrows drawing inward. And… are those tears? Real fucking tears.

Fuck that.

I jostle my hand against her mouth and growl low, "Scream, and I'll go after Jude. I'm going to remove my hand, but only because seeing your tears isn't enough. I want to hear them, too. I want to hear the pain in your voice when you admit to Trenton and Hayes that you fucked them over."

I let go, knowing that where priorities lie, they will always be with her brother and not with Trenton, Hayes… or me.

The tears well deeper in her eyes, masking their color completely. She gasps and chokes, speechless at the camera.

"Remi?" Trenton's voice, shaking and on the brink of losing control, travels through the speaker.

Unable to speak, she whimpers and breaks into sobs. As much as I want to hear her cry, I want to hear and revel in the truth of her twisted words more.

Then… Then we can be done with this damn charade.

Trenton is of a like mind. "Fucking say something!" he yells. Remi jerks, head hitting the trunk of the tree.

An electronic ding bursts through the scene. My attention drops, seeking the source. A notification on her phone? I dart my hand out, wrap it around her backside, and pull the phone from her pocket.

She has the fucking nerve to attempt to yank it out of my hand. I launch backward, swiping the screen on. I realize right away the phone isn't hers, which means it probably belongs to either Porter or Jude.

The message delivered states, "Payment complete." I tap the notification open with my thumb, still holding the recording phone up and pointed at her. She attempts to swipe a second time, and I jerk farther away.

Just when I thought my feelings were as shattered as they could get by finding her actively supporting and participating in this event, the words on the screen prove a heart can break even more: "Street cred goes to you for your kick-ass sleuthing efforts, Remi. Thanks for being my 80 percent - Jude."

Thousands of fucking dollars paid in Remi's name to sell us out. I angle the recording phone down to the shaking hand that's holding yet more proof of her betrayal. Only after I know Trenton and Hayes have seen it, based on the bellow of frustration, do I let her third attempt at stealing the device back be successful.

Her attention drops to the screen. She gasps, chokes over a cry, and covers her mouth, adamantly shaking her head.

"Hope you had fun. Because you are dead to us," I grind out through clenched teeth before stalking away back through the woods.

CHAPTER THIRTY-FOUR

Remi

I collapse, unable to hold myself up. My fingers dig into the earth, begging, pleading with mother nature to give me the strength I need to not simply lie here on the damp, leaf littered ground until someone finds me.

Heaving on my hands and knees, vision blackening at the sides, I focus on my clenched fingers and the cool dirt sifting between them.

The string ring Trenton had given me strains against my tightened knuckles then snaps and falls. The thin, gray strands disappear. I claw madly at the ground, tears blurring my vision and streaking my face, nails embedded with soil, trying desperately to find the memento of something so incredibly amazing that I lost.

Aside from photographs, my bike is the one item I have remaining to remind me of Dad. That silly thin little string is the only item I have — had — to remind me of Trenton, Hayes, and Crow.

Trenton might have been the one who gave it to me, but it represented all of them.

I pound at the earth, pissed that it would choose tonight to steal it from me — the night I managed to break my own heart with my lies and deceit. Again.

It doesn't take long for footsteps to approach. Jude's arms are under me in an instant, lifting me off the ground, while his dark-brown eyes scan my body, my face — everything — for answers. "Who did this to you?" he asks, attention darting toward the curvy road that disappears into the woods.

Unable to speak or express anything at this point, I shake my head. To be honest, I'm not sure what combination of words would be the most fitting for the fucktastic mess I am in.

But then Jude unholsters his gun, the one he always keeps hidden and secured by his waistband, and prowls into the woods.

"No!" I scream, my voice deciding this is the most opportune moment to work.

Jude freezes but not for long enough before he realizes my scream means that the source of my anguish is indeed headed in that direction. His prowl quickly turns into a run.

271

I struggle to stand, spiked heels slipping through the slick leaves and sinking into the earth. Every uplift of my foot gathers dried leaves on my heels like a spear-tipped litter picker collects garbage off the sides of the roads.

When I finally do get my footing, I tug each heel off and dash into a sprint as fast as my bare feet can take me. But by the time I catch up, Jude has found his target.

The two men are nose-to-nose. Jude's gun is pressed firmly against the side of Crow's head, the indentation of the metal clearly visible even in the dark night. I slow my run, quiet my steps, knowing my brother more than I know myself most days.

If I startle him, he might react — shoot first, ask questions later, especially if the person is a threat to family.

If Crow is scared, he is a master at pretending. In fact, he is practically pressing his head against the chamber, daring Jude to make the kill shot. I don't know what frightens me more, his willingness to take a bullet or Jude's willingness to deliver one.

Entire body weak and trembling, I pad lightly in their direction. They're in a low and menacing verbal duel — tones far more frightening than the yelling, passionate type.

I slowly and quietly let my presence be known in their peripherals, knowing that by the time I am right beside them, they both will have likely noticed.

Jude's finger tightens around the trigger, and my chest and throat tighten around a scream, but I choke it down. A heartbeat later, my presence is recognized, and his head jerks my direction, the barrel of the gun digging deeper into Crow's temple to compensate for the distraction.

The distraction is enough to put Jude at a disadvantage. Crow swipes at Jude's arm, and I dive to the ground out of pure preservation instinct, letting the fear drive my body, just like Crow taught me. Thankfully, the gun doesn't go off; Jude is a wild card but not that wild. My head lifts in time to watch Crow put Jude into an arm triangle choke, wrench the gun from him, and press it into Jude's temple instead.

I know Jude. I don't know Crow. Not like I know my brother. Jude could have maybe been talked down. Crow… I have no clue. All I know is he is about to take away my only remaining family

273

and leave me with the one person I want to get the farthest away from — Porter.

"Crow… please…" I beg.

"Shut the fuck up, Remi," he responds, stepping away from Jude who goes tumbling onto the ground and scrambles to stand and face Crow.

Crow aims the gun straight at Jude's head, mere feet separating them. His aim is steady and confident, not revved and shaken by adrenaline and emotion like Jude's was. Crow's opposite hand digs into his pocket just as the sound of crunching leaves and running steps echo around us.

Whatever Crow had planned picks up pace as someone else arrives at the scene. He grapples to finish pulling something up on his phone with one hand while the other adjusts the gun's aim from Jude to our new visitor.

The new confident set in Jude's shoulders as he darts alternating glances over my shoulder and back to Crow proves who it is without the need for me to check.

Porter appears by my side, his own gun drawn, and slowly approaches Crow. My vision caves in — body, mind, soul in a three-way tug of war.

Crow holds the phone out toward Jude, screen vertical. The far-off, electric whir of speeding vehicles caught on camera overrides the local chirp of insects, rumble of vehicles, and din of conversation coming through the trees from the street. Jude steps forward, eyes squinting to get a better look at whatever Crow is showing him.

His attention whips to me and Porter and back to the screen again. Then, Crow flips the phone back around, alternating glances from the line of the gun to Porter and his phone to Jude as he thumbs up something else and flips the screen back around to show Jude.

Hayes's voice floats through my mind. A memory of the night I had "stalkered" Porter: *"He records everything. Incriminating evidence and all that."*

The first video he showed Jude was from when I made Porter crash.

But what is the second one?

CHAPTER THIRTY-FIVE

J ude blanches in the moonlight, and his hands whiten into deadly fists at his sides. Eyes blinking rapidly and Adam's apple repeatedly bobbing over swallows, my brother looks from Porter to me and back again. Crow stuffs his phone away, sidesteps to me, grasps my wrists, and yanks me toward Jude.

Jude and Porter instantly react: Jude snarls at the rough handling, and Porter clicks his safety off. Both men get dangerously close to Crow and me until the four of us are in a tight circle.

Crow lets go of my wrist and holds up his hand, palm vertical in defense. He then moves the same hand in my direction, eyes locked on Jude, gun in the opposite hand still lifted and aimed at Porter. The two of them are in a standoff — one where Porter is concentrating a hell of a lot more than Crow is seeing as Crow's attention is directed at Jude.

His fingers meet my cheek, and I nearly combust into tears on the spot — already missing the type of touch I never truly got from him. He wipes my tears away, grasps my chin, and angles my face toward Jude.

The first words in this showdown are uttered low and confident by Crow: "Tell him, Remi."

Hearing my name fall from his lips when he'd been so engaged in a silent conversation with Jude shocks me out of my stuporous daze.

At first, I'm not entirely sure which lie Crow is expecting me to divulge. At least not until he scoops his fingers around the side of my head behind my ear and drags his thumb over my cheek where it is still sticky from lingering tears. He doesn't just drag it, though, he rubs the spot, using my tears to wipe off any remaining makeup that covers the now-yellowing, almost-healed bruise.

"Say something, Remi," Jude whispers, eyes darting wildly between Porter and me. My mouth gapes open and closed like a fish out of water. Jude's already almost-black eyes darken dangerously, and he pierces me with a glare.

My entire body trembles. The proof I had hoped he would find is right here. Yet the words of said proof — the verbal admission — is still stuck in my throat, unwilling to let go. "I—" I stutter and gasp, breathing turning shallow. Porter... is right next to me; I can feel the warmth of his body seeping into my arm. The threat of his presence. The promise of those threats.

His quiet attendance roars in my head. A pulsating *wop-wop* thuds in my ears. The blood in my veins measures at a fast, erratic beat and consumes all my senses.

Or that's what I thought was happening until Jude's eyes leave mine and drift upward toward a spot in the sky visible between tree tops. Blinking rapidly to clear my tunneling vision, the white, webbed glow of a search light spans the sky.

The *wop-wop* wasn't just my pulse but the rhythmic blades of a helicopter.

Someone must've reported the meet.

"Shit," Jude whispers.

"Tell him, Remi!" Crow growls, the low pitch eerily similar to the rumble of the chopper.

"Yeah, Remi... tell him. Tell Jude everything," Porter chides with a huff and an eye roll, switching from one foot to the other and tightening his fingers over the gun's grip.

Jude's attention flashes between us, battling with whom to award the most attention. "Porter, go get everyone out of here," he instructs.

Porter's eyes flick around our group, and he swallows hard but otherwise doesn't argue. Jaw set, he gives Jude a sharp nod and backs away slowly.

When Porter turns around and jogs back toward the event, Crow lets go of my face with a growl of frustration.

Jude holds his hand out, requesting Crow give him his gun back. Out of good faith, Crow hands it over. He accomplished what he could. His job here — whatever it was exactly — is done.

Once Jude's gun is holstered, he turns to me. Crow slinks off into the darkness.

"Someone is taking the blame for this tonight," he states matter-of-factly, fingers brushing away the wisps of hair stuck to my cheek. "You get to choose who."

My knees can scarcely keep me erect. If… If only it were that easy. Porter's threat just moments ago was loud and clear. As was every threat before that from the one on my cheek to all the invisible ones. I am done being his plaything, though. I was done the moment I left him at the line when Crow took me here to ride WOT on the very road through these trees.

I made a promise. To Crow, yes. But mostly to myself. I might keep secrets, but I don't break promises. Everyone keeps secrets, after all. No one is immune.

Promises… are sacred.

Even still, admitting the truth is hard. Porter is smart. He could find a way to counter any- and everything I might accuse him of. Jude trusts him; convincing my brother that the man he trusts more than any other is abusing and threatening his little sister is so much harder than it seems.

Porter can debunk me. He can spill honeyed words to make me come across as melodramatic. He can take advantage of the fact that we used to be an item — that once upon a time, I consented to having him in my bed.

"I…" God just say something, Remi. Anything. Steeling my shoulders, lifting my chin, and sucking in a breath, I force words to fall from my tongue, "You wo—" My revelation is shattered, when two sets of headlights appear through the trees from the direction in which Crow left.

Jude grabs my arm and pulls me deeper into the woods, squinting at the bright lights. When he realizes they aren't cops, his tense shoulders loosen, and his grip on my arm slackens.

One of the cars I don't recognize, but the second one, I do. My heart collides with my ribcage. The circular headlights of a familiar Bimmer come into view. Hayes slams to a stop, rolls the windows down, leans out, and pitches his voice into the dense pines. "Remi?"

Jude looks down at me and back up again.

"I know you are right here somewhere. Listen to me," Hayes continues. "Trust me. Whatever you do, do not say anything else. Do not admit to anything." The advice comes across adamant, his voice tight and clipped. Considering I know they want me to come clean about Porter, this counsel doesn't make any sense. But the insistence is coated in a desperate fervor that can't be ignored.

Jude's hand moves to his gun, but I wrap my fingers around his wrist and wordlessly beg him to let go. "They are not the ones you need to be wary of, Jude," I state, hoping I am not wrong.

Jude's jaw moves over clenched teeth. He lets go of his gun, but then… Then, he stalks away — away from me, back toward the event, taking what's left of my already shattered heart with him.

The tears well up and pour over so copiously and so fast, it's almost as though they were never dammed to begin with.

One of the guys' arms wrap around me, and he helps me to stand. "We need to get out of here, Remi. Our indemnity only works under certain parameters, and being at this meet, in the woods, does not fall under those parameters. Where's your bike?" Hayes asks.

I sniffle. "At home. I rode here with Jude."

"Good." He guides me to the Bimmer. Crow and Trenton are in some sort of heated discussion. When I get closer, their discussion stops, and their gazes land on me through the open windows. Hard and cold. Not at all welcoming. My feet become lead, attempting to halt me on the spot as Hayes works to drive me forward.

Something is wrong. These are not the sweet, fun guys I got to know.

Crow jumps out of the car at the same time I turn myself into a noodle, slip out of Hayes's arms, and shamble to get away.

"Nice try, Remi," Crow growls, arm wrapping around my midsection. He shoves me toward the car and presses my head under the frame to push me inside.

Trenton is now beside me in the back seat. Waiting. When I attempt to scamper out, his arm clamps around my wrist, and he tugs me back inside so Crow can shut the door, imprisoning me.

Crow leans his forearms on the window ledge and dips his head down, tattooed fingers dangling inside like he doesn't have a care in the world.

"You have a shit ton of explaining to do," Trenton whispers in my ear.

Crow raises an eyebrow at me and drags his upper teeth along his labret piercing. "Where are you taking her?" he asks Hayes, his tone rushed as he darts a glance through the trees toward the maniacally dispersing event.

Hayes turns around in the driver seat and puts the Bimmer into gear. "The shipping port."

CHAPTER THIRTY-SIX

Jude

Porter is collecting the markers while the remaining roaches scatter. Uncaring that the cops are coming, I stalk up to him, swing back the butt of my gun and knock him out cold. Best friend or not, blood runs thicker. Especially when it comes to my sister.

I hate that she could never say the words. But she didn't have to. What I saw on that second video was enough.

Knowing he has been treating Remi inappropriately sends a rage through me unlike anything I have ever experienced. I got a taste of it when I assumed that Crow guy was at fault. But having it end up being Porter is worse. So much damn worse.

He crumples to the ground, and I drag him over to my car. Since he is nearly twice my weight — and dead weight at that — it's only through sheer force and determination that I manage to disarm and load him into the back seat. After tossing his gun into my glovebox, I hop into the driver's seat while simultaneously trying to dial his number from my cell.

Come on, Remi. Answer.

No answer comes. I hang up on the voicemail and try again. Still no answer.

Wasting no more time, I drop the phone into my lap and speed into the woods, figuring since those guys clearly got here this way, we must be able to get out this way, too.

As soon as there's nothing more to worry about but getting from point A to point B, I prop my elbow up on the center console and train my gun on an unconscious Porter.

That conversation with Remi and her... friends?... is not over. Nor is the one with Porter. But first, I need to find them. To do that, I drive straight to the house in search of her cellphone so I can access their phone numbers and maybe do a reverse search.

Getting home doesn't take much time when running all the lights and weaving in and out of traffic. Porter, thankfully, stays passed out the entire ride.

When I pull onto the street, though, there is a car parked directly across from our house. Lights off. The same car in the woods. The one belonging to that Crow guy.

Unsure how to manage Porter and still accomplish what I need to do, I pull into the carport, jump out, and grab a rope and old shop rag from the garage.

Using both items, I bind and gag Porter so he can't get away while I'm doing a little sleuthing of my own.

Remi had said she left her phone on my bed, so that is the first direction I take, entering through the downstairs door and turning each corner slowly, knowing damn well that guy is here… somewhere. Gun cocked and ready, I let the barrel precede my every step.

I make it inside my room and turn my bed and side table inside out trying to find her phone, but it's not here. A quiet creak sounds above my head, and I dart a glance up. The sound comes from Remi's room. Dude must think he's being a sneaky fucker by taking slow, careful steps.

Before checking the upper level, I slip into Porter's room on the off chance her phone is in there.

When I don't have any luck finding it in there either, I head upstairs next, taking each step slowly and silently before whipping my gun and focusing into the living room once at the top.

My eyes drift to Dad's chair, and my lips twitch at the corners. As quietly as possible, I approach the leather judge seat and sit down, easing back so as not to trigger the sound of leather rubbing.

Then… I wait, gun propped on my knee and aimed toward the corner where the fireplace room and hallway converge.

As soon as the dark figure steps a steel-toed boot past the threshold, I release the safety, gladly allowing the eerie echo of metal clicking to float through the room. He freezes, one foot in my sightline, the rest of him hidden behind the wall that serves as a temporary barrier.

CHAPTER THIRTY-SEVEN

Remi

We drive all the way through the beach side of the county and on toward town in complete silence. Tension in the cab is thick and muggy. When we cross the bridge, I assume they must be taking me back to their place, but instead of turning left at the light, they take a right into the port Hayes and I had spoken about that night we all hung out at the marina.

My heart doubles its efforts and a sheen of sweat covers my forehead as I note all the units, blinding lights, and bustle of late-night work crews. I close my eyes and practice drawing in long, deep breaths — in through my nose, out through my mouth.

Hayes weaves through a good portion of the hundreds-of-acres of concrete and metal until we reach a large warehouse.

Terminal warehouses are already quite large, but it appears this one is being expanded to be even bigger. Hayes loops around to the part that's still under construction and drives directly under the maw of beams and trusses until we're in the several-thousand-square-foot building.

It's the only place that doesn't seem to have people working — the only place where we won't be watched. Though I know plenty of workers saw us enter, every one of them turned a blind eye at our arrival.

Perhaps that night on the marina, I should have asked Hayes what he and the guys knew about water vessels instead of the other way around.

Once parked, no one seems particularly eager to be the first to speak, so we all get out of the stuffy car in silence and situate ourselves on a nearby crate.

Trenton, oftentimes the icebreaker, finally speaks up: "This night can go one of two ways, Remi. Either in your favor or against it. The choice is yours."

Under most circumstances one might consider themselves lucky to hold the power of choice. For me, this is not one of those circumstances. A bitterness coats my tongue.

During the ride, I had inched myself away from Trenton until my back was pressed against the rear passenger door. Out here on this crate, I choose to keep away, too. He doesn't encourage me closer nor does he close the distance of his own accord.

Do I blame him? Not at all.

"Who are you really, and what is your involvement with this new club?" Hayes asks.

There is no sense in beating around the bush any longer. I had tried to protect both sides — tried to prevent something like this happening all while still keeping a modicum of self-preservation. Clearly none of it worked, and now I'm a newly resurrected piece in a figurative game of checkers, acting as a king's crown — back on the game board and changing the rules.

Except I don't feel very majestic.

More like a pawn.

Everything — yet nothing — has changed.

I steel my shoulders and take a cleansing breath, drawing in any and all the confidence I can. Then... I tell them everything.

Well, almost. Tonight, I'm all about being honest and coming clean, but there are still some things that should not be discussed.

Even if I am technically not sharing anything they don't already know — or have at least surmised

— a tremendous weight lifts from my shoulders as the words begin to pour out. "My name is Remi-Sue Delancey," I explain. "Formerly, and for most of my life, known as Sue — or Suzi. Daughter of Troy Delancey, previous owner of Lance Industries."

I let that one, bold statement settle. Hayes doesn't look surprised, but Trenton's eyebrows rise sky high, and he blinks, repeatedly alternating glances between Hayes and me. "Lance Industries practically owns the West Coast."

"And will eventually monopolize the automotive industry on the East Coast, too. At least, that's the long-term goal," I add matter-of-factly. There is no need for me to detail what Lance Industries is all about because anyone who knows vehicles, knows the size, shape, and flavors of pies that make up Lance Industries. I continue by answering the second part of their inquiry: "As you probably realize by now, the crew tonight is run by Porter and my brother, Jude. I want absolutely nothing to do with it. None of it. Not the company, not the crew. In short, Porter tied my hands."

"In short?" Trenton huffs. "That man… did a hell of a lot more than tie your hands, Remi."

"You think I don't know that!?" I lash out, narrowing a glare at him. "Listen. I get that you guys are pissed off — that you don't understand my angle. But I will not be bullied or pressured. Not when I'm only just now Houdini-ing myself out of the straight-jacket in which Porter had me bound."

Hayes visibly relaxes, but his head falls back and hand drags over his face. "We want to help you, Remi. Not corner you. But we can't do that if you keep lying to us."

My heart drops to the pit of my stomach. "I know. I'm mostly an open book, but there is… some confidentiality involved when it comes to certain things. Just like with Revelry and The Gulf Coasters — there was plenty you didn't tell me in the beginning, and plenty more I have yet to learn."

"Why were you there tonight if you wanted nothing to do with the crew or the races?" Trenton asks with a mix between a contained choke and growl.

I do my absolute best to explain everything that went down at home after I went back: my decision to not choose either crew; How Porter lingered; Jude's honest request for moral support. "I love Jude more than anything in the entire world. I don't have to agree with what he is doing, but you all need to understand that he is my everything. He's all the family I have left." My throat, nose, and eyes burn, but I manage to keep a cry from tearing its way past my tongue.

Trenton finally comes closer. His hand reaches out and fingers push along my jaw.

"I love my brother… but I really like you guys, too," I choke out on a whisper. "Please don't make me choose."

Tears prick at the corner of my eyes as I lean my cheek into Trenton's palm. His sepia gaze scans my face and dark-blond eyebrows curve inward, but there's a bite to both his tone and his fingers. "You'll choose your brother. That much is already clear."

A sob catches in my throat. There is no denying that fact, even if my heart aches at the thought of losing Trenton, Crow, and Hayes in the process. My watery focus travels toward Hayes. He's watching me with an inquisitive glare, fingers clenching into a bundle of papers at his side.

I swallow the salty emotions and remove Trenton's hand from my face.

"Okay," Hayes sighs, darting a glare at Trenton. Trenton's lips press into a fine line. I decide that I don't like this version of him — the bad cop that Hayes had warned me about. "Let's continue with what you just said about Porter. About him tying your hands. All these instances of abuse lately…" Hayes is very precise and cautious with his approach to the topic. "When you say he tied your hands, are you indicating that he was threatening you? Dictating your actions?"

Hayes means well. I know they have seen Porter do underhanded and shady things in real life. They've seen the bruising and accepted me with open arms when I was at my lowest, so this question comes as no surprise.

But never once have I had to form words — to verbally sit on the stand and testify to Porter's behavior. Opening up about something so scary and so dangerous is really, really damn difficult.

I go on to explain what I was "hired" to do and how skillfully Porter kept me on track. "I found you guys immediately — the night I showed up at The Crow Bar and Grill, riding my bicycle."

Trenton's eyes close and his chest rises and falls, trembling over a pained, controlled breath. Hayes had warned me about his temper, but this is the first time I have ever witnessed him attempt to keep it under control.

Meeting Trenton that night was… everything. I just hope that while he's pulling the particulars of my betrayal, he remembers everything in between, too. The proof they want is in all the little details:

My bruised cheek.

My delayed text response that night.

My shoe laces covered in sand spurs because I had to sneak out.

When his gaze pierces mine again, I plead wordlessly with my eyes that he just try. Try to read between all the lines of our story.

Hayes watches this back and forth in silence. When it's clear neither of us are going to say anything, he continues. "Right. So he was using you as a weapon, a spy, to get information about us?"

"Yeah. But, see, that's just the thing. I never actually gave them any useful information. Not once."

"We want to believe you, but this doesn't look good. You understand that, right?" Hayes asks.

I give a small nod, teeth nibbling on the inside of my cheek as I think everything through.

Hayes takes a deep breath. "We knew Crow was going to check on you, but only because when he says he needs a drink, that often means he's about to do something reckless that has nothing to do with getting wasted. As soon as we found him, he told us he showed Jude the videos he had taken that night. We worried he might do that and hoped to stop him, but we were too late."

"Both the videos he showed him were from the same night? I know the first one was of the race and crash, but wh-what was the second one?"

We did a lot that night.

At the marina.

In the bedroom.

"The second one was of Porter harassing you in the parking lot at the pier. It's the only proof we have. Porter didn't get rough enough that time for it to be incriminating, and Crow stopped the video short in order to step in before he did."

Jude hadn't given any indicator that the video helped him understand the dynamic of the situation between Porter and me.

Not too long after that, I had almost worked up the nerve to reveal something, but Hayes and Trenton rolled up at that very moment. "Why did you want to stop Crow from telling Jude about Porter?"

Something is not adding up. Not at all. My focus darts from both men. Trenton is still keyed up — still trying to rein in his emotions. Something about this comment doesn't sit right with him — the fingers on his lap that were already loose, but twitchy, start to curl.

Hayes slides the stack of papers he had been holding onto the crate between us, but before I can look, Trenton snatches them up and sets them down behind his back. He lifts a finger and opens his mouth to say something for the first time in the past several minutes, but Hayes gives Trenton a warning press against his chest-shoulder area.

Trenton's eyebrows flatten, face reddens, and he clenches his teeth so hard I fear they'll bust. Whatever point he was hoping to bring up is further thwarted by the blinding lights of an approaching vehicle.

Trenton jumps to his feet to stand beside Hayes, their bodies forming a barricade between me and whoever has chosen this moment to appear.

Since I can't see, and therefore can't be worried or excited with who has arrived, my mind homes in on the fact that even though clearly Trenton doesn't trust me and is upset, he still cares.

They had both blocked me, but Trenton's arm shot behind his back, seeking me out without contact, and he even stayed a step or two behind Hayes, unwilling to get too far away.

Stealing the moment of opportunity, I inch forward and grab his hand. His fingers tighten around mine and squeeze, using my touch as an anchor just as much as I am using his.

"Shit," Hayes mumbles, quickly turning to face me. "All the answers about why we didn't want Jude to find out about Porter are in those documents. But, unfortunately, we don't have time to go over that right now. As much as I would like to stick Porter with every single accusation he likely deserves, this is one of those rare instances where secrets are better kept buried. For now."

Peeking around Trenton's arm, I spot the problem: Jude's GT-R rolls into the warehouse. I let go of Trenton's hand and step past his side despite their efforts to protect me. After all, Jude is my brother, and I know for a fact that he would never cause me harm.

When he passes under the first beam of temporary construction lighting, an outline in the passenger seat can be seen. One that, at a quick glance, doesn't look at all like Porter, but quite the opposite. Black to his strawberry-blond; fair to his golden tan.

My assessment is confirmed, however, when both doors open and two men exit. One of whom is most certainly not Porter. My eyes bug wide at being witness to swarthy Crow stepping out of the passenger side of Jude's pristine, light-gold "Silica Breath" Skyline. One, because it very much does not suit him, and two, because he… He is riding with my brother. I can't decide if I should find it amusing or terrifying.

Trenton and Hayes seem equally as surprised and perplexed. The surprises don't end there, though. Both newly-arrived men circle around and meet at the passenger side, pop the front seat, and drag out a fighting and writhing… Porter.

It's a damn party…

CHAPTER THIRTY-EIGHT

Porter is only partially of a sane mind. He is bloodied and bruised, bound by rope and gagged. No matter how much I have grown to dislike the man, I can't stop my hand from covering my mouth to stifle the gasp as Crow and Jude drag Porter toward us and unceremoniously sling him to a rest against one of the nearby crates.

Jude stoops to his haunches, whips out his gun, and presses it against Porter's temple. "Move, make a sound, or even so much as accidentally tip over, and you'll regret it."

Porter's eyes widen even despite how woozy he is. He might know more about finances and whatever the CFO of a company does, but he is not at all ignorant about what Jude is capable of. Relationships be damned.

But, hell, what did Crow and Jude do to him? And how did that unlikely pair come to be together?

Apparently in this moment, those details don't matter. Crow approaches Hayes and Trenton, and Jude approaches me.

Jude's eyes are frenzied. I have only ever seen them this way once. Usually by the time he's interacting with me, whatever scenario kicked in his frenetic adrenaline is fading or long gone. Right now, though, he is in the midst of the insanity.

I have always known my brother to be a little crazy. But some days it's hard to believe it with as socially respectable as he is. Just like Dad. They could turn stuff like this on or off like a light switch.

I slip my arms around his waist and press my head against his chest, hoping to bring back a little of his humanity. It seems to work. He at least has the sense to holster his gun before wrapping his arms around me and squeezing tight.

His chest moves raggedly under my head as he sucks in a deep breath — one of recovery that he probably hadn't dared take in a while if there was any sort of agenda he'd been trying to accomplish. "Remi, I still don't know what the fuck is going on, but I saw enough."

I squeeze him tighter. "Jude…" I whisper, heart rapping so hard I fear a heart attack will take me before the words I hope he has enough mental capacity to absorb fall from my mouth. "There's so much you don't know. Some of which you will never forgive me for. As for Porter? If you knew the entire truth about what he has done to me, he would have been dead by your hand a long time ago."

The only way to get those words out is to dump them like a waterfall of milk into a bowl of cereal. If I hesitate or overthink, he would never hear them. Even still, I admit the truth without exact words. Even still, I lie… by reserving details better left private. Forever. Because even if Porter was already in the grave, the truth of what he has done to me would make Jude want to kill someone else, just to let out some aggression.

I no longer regret my secrets. I do not regret my choice to slowly drip details to everyone involved. Yes, it's hard. Yes, it hurts. Yes, it takes more bravery than honesty. But some things are never meant to be spoken, no matter how ethical or right one might consider the need for said information.

Jude inches back and scans me from head to toe, his jaw set in a tight line. "Right now, I am not going to ask, because, according to your friend, Crow, I probably shouldn't kill Porter. Yet." He digs my phone out of his pocket and holds it out for me to collect. "It was in the office."

So Porter was definitely the culprit.

Surprise, surprise.

I retrieve Porter's phone from my back pocket, hand it to Jude, and shove mine in there instead. "Yeah... that's the best idea. Crow... He's a smart guy." I choke a little on the words, my gaze flitting over Jude's shoulder to the subject of our conversation.

Crow's eyes are already on me, his palm over his mouth and chin as his chrome eyes pierce me from under those black, spider-like lashes. As soon my gaze catches his, though, he looks away, returning to the more intense and important conversation Revelry appears to be having.

Jude nods, somehow understanding all the implied words I want to convey, but then his expression of understanding drops and transforms to one of a deep-seated pain and regret. The transformation of his features is so overwhelming, so heartbreaking, my hands launch to his arms and I squeeze, shaking him a little.

His eyes redden, which is not an easy task to accomplish for him, and he blinks violently. "Remi... Remi... Oh my God. I... I'm sorry I was so damn blind. How long?"

I shake my head. No way in hell am I giving him that information. His jaw tightens again, and a single tear breaks free, tracking down to the cliff of his jaw before dropping onto my forearm. So much of who my brother is deep, deep down is revealed in such a small token.

Jude blinks any remaining, potential tears away and clears his throat. "You know what?" he whispers low, giving me a watery chuckle. "If he poked you too hard in the ribs or if he beat and defiled you, it doesn't matter which end of the spectrum…" His voice changes to something that would frighten anyone into an early death. "His place is in the grave."

Every single hair on my arms becomes erect with the muttered promise.

"But first, we have to fix whatever-the-fuck he screwed up. Because all damn signs point to the fact that he has done more than just screw my sister. And I need him alive to get the details.

TO BE CONTINUED

ABOUT THE AUTHOR

Adell Ryan is a hubby/wife pseudonym. Adell writes unconventional love stories about fierce women and their numerous male suitors. Because let's be honest, we need more than one to satisfy our multi-dimensional needs. Right? Ryan simply puts up with Adell's crazy fantasies and toots her horn regularly. Occasionally he'll add in a shoulder pat, and a deep, sexy "Damn that's good stuff."

That southern boy (bless him) stole this northern girl's heart and they live together in the deep south, raising their three boys. When Adell isn't writing she's homeschooling — primarily working on dictation, making sure they say 'creek' instead of 'crick' and 'fire' instead of 'fer.' She also dabbles in photography and graphic design. Oh yeah, and reading. Every. Night. Much to Ryan's dismay. Sometimes she puts the steamy stuff down and gives him a quick kiss on the forehead though.

To be the *first* to know about new releases and exclusive behind-the-scenes stuff, join the fun in her FB Group: facebook.com/groups/authoradellryan/
You can also check out her website at https://www.adellryan.com and sign-up for her newsletter.
Still not enough? Find her at the listed social media platforms as well!:

| Goodreads | Instagram | Pinterest |
| BookBub | Twitter | Patreon |

Printed in Great Britain
by Amazon

42285968R00169